A Haunted Year

Ann Phillips

Macmillan Publishing Company
New York

Maxwell Macmillan International
New York   Oxford   Singapore   Sydney

First American edition 1994
Text copyright © 1991 by Ann Phillips
Afterword copyright © 1994 by Ann Phillips
Illustrations copyright © 1994 by Teresa Flavin
Macmillan Publishing Company is part of the
Maxwell Communication Group of Companies.
Macmillan Publishing Company
866 Third Avenue
New York, NY 10022
First published by Oxford University Press, Oxford, England
Printed in the United States of America
10   9   8   7   6   5   4   3   2   1
The text of this book is set in 12 point Goudy Old Style.

Library of Congress Cataloging-in-Publication Data
Phillips, Ann.
A haunted year / Ann Phillips. — 1st American ed.
p.   cm.
Summary: In 1910 in England, Florence summons up the ghost of George, a twelve-
year-old half-French cousin, and tries to hide him from the rest of the household.
ISBN 0-02-774605-4
[1. Ghosts—Fiction. 2. Cousins—Fiction. 3. England—Fiction.]
I. Title.
PZ7.P5255Hau 1994   92-45638
[Fic]—dc20

THE GAGE FAMILY

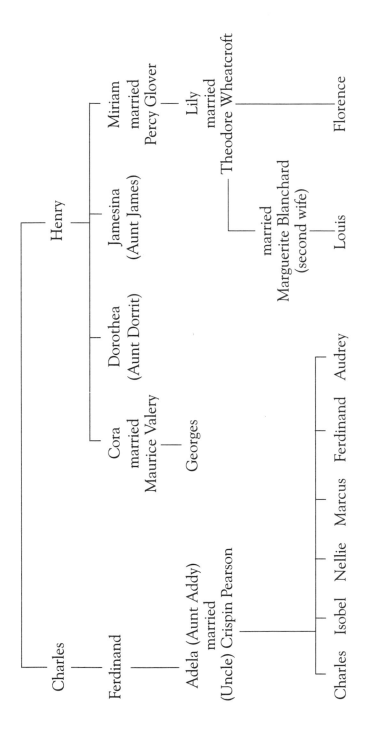

THE OUTLANDISH KNIGHT

"An outlandish knight from the north land came,
And he came wooing of me;
And he told me he'd take me to that northern land,
And there he would marry me."

"Well, go and get me some of your father's gold,
And some of your mother's fee,
And two of the very best stable steeds,
Where there stand thirty and three."

She borrowed some of her father's gold,
And some of her mother's fee,
And away they did go to the stable door,
Where horses stood thirty and three.

She mounted on her lily-white horse,
And he upon the gray,
And away they did ride to the fair riverside,
Three hours before it was day.

He says: "Unlight, my little Polly,
Unlight, unlight," cries he,
"For six pretty maids I've drowned here before,
And the seventh thou art to be.

"Pull off, pull off your silken gown,
And deliver it unto me,
For I think it's too fine and much too gay
To rot in the saltwater sea."

She said: "Go get a sickle to crop the thistle
That grows beside the brim,
That it may not mingle with my curly locks,
Nor harm my lily-white skin."

So he got a sickle to crop the thistle,
That grew beside the brim,
She catched him around the middle so small,
And tumbled him into the stream.

"Lie there, lie there, you false-hearted man,
Lie there instead of me,
For six pretty maidens thou hast drowned here before,
And the seventh has drowned thee."

Then she mounted on her lily-white horse,
And she did ride away,
And she arrived at her father's stable door
Three hours before it was day.

Now the parrot being in the window so high,
A-hearing the lady, he did say:
"I'm afraid that some ruffian have led you astray,
That you've tarried so long away."

"Don't prittle, don't prattle, my pretty Polly,
Nor tell no tales of me,
And your cage shall be of the glittering gold,
And your perch of the best ivory."

Now the master being in the bedroom so high,
A-hearing the parrot he did say:
"What's the matter with you, my pretty Polly,
You're prattling so long before day?"

"There come an old cat on top of my cage,
To take my sweet life away.
I was just calling on my young mistress
To drive that old puss away."

—Traditional English Ballad

PART ONE

Late March to Late May 1910
at the Paragon

1

Florence did not invent George, though many people afterward suggested that she had and Louis accused her of it outright. She found George; and the first thing she found was his photograph in an old gray album with silk tassels on the strings that tied its pages.

His photograph was a faded sepia, but even from the pale brown his face stood out—dark-eyed, dark-haired, smiling with a hint of challenge. He was the only child (except for fat important babies) on the crowded pages and he looked about twelve or so—an interesting age to Florence.

"Who's this boy?" she asked at once.

Both her aunts looked up from their reading (it was Sunday afternoon, and in 1910 reading was about all that you could properly do on a Sunday—apart from actually going to church; sewing or playing games were not thought right at all). Florence carried the album over to them.

The temperature in the stuffy room suddenly seemed to chill. "Oh dear me!" said stout Aunt James; Aunt Dorrit, the bony one, merely said "Hmm!"

"Can't you remember?" asked Florence.

Aunt James said "No" and Aunt Dorrit said "Yes" and they both looked embarrassed and confused.

"Who was it then?" begged Florence. "Can't you see properly? Shall I draw the curtains?" Curtains closed to keep out even pale sunshine were also part of Sunday afternoon, and the light in the room was greenish and swimmy.

"It's George, dear. We don't speak of him," said Aunt Dorrit.

"Best forgotten. Years ago, anyway," said Aunt James.

Florence sensed a mystery. "Do tell," she urged. "Please! He's only a boy. What happened to him?"

"It's all forgotten," said Aunt Dorrit firmly; but although she sounded brisk, she shivered and drew the lace closer around her neck. "He lived in France, anyway," she added. "He was half French: not *George*, really, but *Georges*. He had a French father. And that's all."

"All?" said Florence. "Aren't there stories about him? What did he do?"

"Nothing anybody remembers," said Aunt James, stiff. "No more questions, Florence. We want to read."

"I shall ask my father when he comes home," said Florence, stifling her disappointment.

"Do, dear," said both aunts cordially. And Florence could get no more out of them. She brooded over the picture of the boy in his dark jersey and noticed G. *Valery* in ink under the photograph, faintly written. She slid off her upright chair (the horsehair in the stuffing of the seat had come through in places, and was scratchy at the backs of her knees) and went to the writing table by the window. Both aunts read studiously, determinedly oblivious of her.

Florence pulled open the drawer of the table and rummaged inside. Pens—sealing wax—a seal ring—a paperweight—a page of pins—various scraps, letters, cuttings—and, yes, a small silver penknife with initials engraved on the handle. G.V.

"Can I borrow George's knife?" asked Florence casually.

"Borrow what you like," said Aunt Dorrit. Her voice was vague, but her eyes looked sharply.

"The things in there are your father's," added Aunt James.

Florence put the knife in her pinafore pocket, smiled innocently at the aunts, and went off to her bedroom.

2

In the most secret place in the garden, behind Mr. Creed the gardener's greenhouse, Florence had made a circle of stones in the wide gravel path. The stones were close-set, each touching its neighbor, and were all white. The circle was big enough for two people to stand in. In the middle of it Florence laid on the ground the photograph of Georges, which she had prized off its page in the album while her aunts were out, and on top of it the silver knife, open. The strong breeze caught at the photograph but the knife held it down, a prisoner.

Florence stood in the circle. She had heard of magic circles; she felt quite sure what to do. She held up her arms and looked at the sky, where high white clouds ran fast before the wind.

"Come here, George," she said. "I want you here. Please, George. Come."

She shut her eyes and bent her head toward the ground. When she opened her eyes again she was looking at a pair of boots. Not her own boots, which were brown and scuffed and topped by long white socks, but black ones, shining, topped by gray ribbed socks and, at knee level, blue serge knickerbockers. George, dark-haired, bright-eyed, was standing beside her in the ring.

"Well?" he said, and laughed. "So? You wanted me to come. Do you want to play?"

Florence laughed too, breathlessly. "Are you really George?" she said. "How old are you?"

"Georges," said the boy. He pronounced it the French way, with soft *g*'s. "How old do you think?"

"About twelve," said Florence.

"About," George agreed. "What shall we do?"

"I'll show you the garden," said Florence: proud, a hostess.

"I know the garden," said George. "I've been here, to see my aunts."

"Dorrit and James—are they your aunts too? Then we're cousins!" said Florence.

"That's why they had my photograph," said George. "They must be your great-aunts, though. Is Lily your mother?"

"My mother's dead," said Florence. She still could not say it matter-of-factly, and had a job to keep her voice flat. "She was called Lily."

"You've got my knife," said George.

Florence pounced on it, and put both knife and photograph into the pocket of her skirt. "I'm keeping it," she said. "It was in the house. The Paragon's my father's house now. He bought it when the aunts couldn't afford to keep it on."

"Where's your father? Is he here?" George asked.

"In Italy," said Florence. "He's working there. He's found some paintings nobody knew about, in an old church. He's an art historian."

"Let's play," said George. "Hide-and-seek. I'll hide."

"Not too near the house," said Florence. "Mr. Creed's gone home, and the aunts are out—but they'll be coming back, and Mrs. Peabody and Hannah are there."

"Still Mrs. Peabody!" said George. "Hannah I don't know."

"I'm counting," said Florence. "One—two—"

George's footfalls went dead as he ran onto grass.

3

It was the Easter holidays for Florence. Normally, school holidays were boredom itself for her. Sometimes school friends came to her, or she went to their houses; but this was not very often. Florence understood, although nobody ever said as much, that her friends' mothers did not really approve of the aunts; and it was true that the aunts were unsociable. They didn't devote their afternoons to visiting, like other elderly ladies; they were too busy painting—Aunt James in the attic, Aunt Dorrit in the conservatory. They had their work.

So did Mrs. Peabody, the cook-housekeeper—always hot, always breathless; so did Hannah, the sixteen-year-old maid, perpetually harried by Mrs. Pea to greater efforts of scrubbing and polishing.

And now Florence had George. Whenever she felt safe from the eyes of Mr. Creed she ran to the secret place behind the greenhouse and whistled to George, and George always came. From behind the syringa hedge, from through the lilacs: He always came at once, smiling and quiet, eager to play. They made their own secret call: a tune of their own invention, which they named the Call Song and sang or whistled to each other as a summoning.

Sometimes it was George who whistled to Florence, but seldom. In the early days, he usually just came when called. Florence never asked him where he came from or went to: She had a feeling that she ought not to—that George would feel the question was an intrusion, and that to know the answer would be upsetting to her herself. She was just satisfied that when Mr. Creed went home, George would be there at her whistle and their games of hiding and chasing could begin. She became very much aware of Mr. Creed's comings and goings. Most days, Monday to Friday, he came to the Paragon at ten and worked till three-thirty, when he went home. Florence and George used to the full the time before ten and after three-thirty. Saturdays and Sundays were their gala days—and the few days when Mr. Creed's rheumatism was playing him up.

Wet days they hated. Mr. Creed lurked in the potting shed or greenhouse, never settling down in the way they liked to a long job of digging or hoeing. And the aunts were liable to erupt into the garden at any moment, in macintoshes down to their ankles, galoshes, and homemade, wide-brimmed waterproof hats. Rain made it too dark for painting, so they gardened instead, unworried by drips down the neck and draggled skirts. Once Florence saw Aunt Dorrit pruning the roses while Aunt James held an umbrella over her head. Mr. Creed disapproved thoroughly of their meddling in his garden and told them that they would get the rheumatics themselves, powerful bad and desperate agonizing. The aunts, well pickled in oil paint and varnish, glue and turpentine, went unscathed.

Wet or dry, Florence and George chased and played in near silence, stifling their giggles; barefoot when the grass was dry enough, otherwise running as lightly as they could, trying to minimize the pounding of their boots—jumping the gravel paths, occasionally landing in flower beds. Their feet were much of a size: Florence was blamed for all the footprints, as well as for the moving of the whitewashed edging stones. Her relationship with Mr. Creed became a tricky one.

She and George were wrapped up in their games, absorbed with an intensity that left Florence no room to ask whether she was happy or miserable. When they had finished teaching each other the games one or the other already knew, they made up one of their own. It was called The Kingdom, and involved a perpetual escape on their part from the enemies of the kingdom they jointly ruled. Mr. Creed, the aunts, callers to the house—everybody was some kind of hunter from whom they ran and hid, scuffling into shrubberies, diving through hedges, crouching under or in low-branched trees. Mr. Creed became the sinister Chancellor, the aunts the wicked Dukes. Life was all an ambush, scary, breathtaking.

How long could it last? Florence wondered every night in the few minutes before she fell dreamlessly asleep. Surely in another day George must be discovered. Surely it would be tomorrow? But the holidays wore on and the high bank of lilacs and syringa between kitchen garden and croquet lawn hid the ever-escaping "king" and "queen" and muffled their laughter with its leaves.

One day, however, Mr. Creed arrived in the breakfast room soon after ten. The aunts had not begun work, as the sky was stormy.

"A word, please, mum," said Mr. Creed, addressing both aunts as one person. Each put down her half of the newspaper. Florence, who had come in for a new boot-lace and was standing on one leg while she threaded it, put her bare foot down and stared at him apprehensively.

"There's been a boy in the garden, mum," said Mr. Creed. "What I don't know is if you know about him. Miss Florence asked him in, but it wasn't one of the young gentlemen I've seen before."

Florence was shocked at how easily the lie came to her. "It was, Mr. Creed," she said innocently. "It was Reggie. You know Reggie Wellington." Among her friends, only two boys ever called at the house, and Dick Dunn, the other one, had butter-colored hair.

"Excusing me, Miss Florence, but plain as plain you called him George," said Mr. Creed. "And don't say as I'm deaf, now. My ears is as sharp as when I was your age."

"Oh well, of course," said Florence. "We play kings and queens. He's King George; I have to be Queen Victoria, although she's dead. Naturally I call him George."

"And footprints. In the rose beds," said Mr. Creed. "I suppose you'll say as you made them all, Miss Florence; but I know your Mr. Reggie was thereabouts."

"Thank you very much, Creed," said Aunt Dorrit in her good-bye voice. "We'll talk to Miss Florence about it."

Mr. Creed went off with an unsatisfied look.

"Now, Florence," said Aunt James briskly. "Reggie? Or George?"

"It really is a game, Aunt James," said Florence, grateful that the truth was so convenient. "Kings and queens. As I said."

The aunts eyed her darkly. "Very well, Florence," said Aunt Dorrit. "We've no objection to Reginald; a nice-mannered lad. But see you tell us when he comes. We should be pleased to see him, and he should be given tea when he comes. Or at least lemonade and a cake."

"Yes, Aunt," said Florence, and escaped thankfully. Mr. Creed was, she saw, in his potting shed. She slid behind the yew trees to where she had left George; he was there, sitting on a bed of dry leaves, his arms clasping his humped knees.

"Mr. Creed is on to you," she whispered.

"Foul spying Chancellor," muttered George.

"I mean really," said Florence. "He's seen you, and he heard me call you George."

"Oh la la!" said George. He didn't appear to take the matter at all seriously. "And what did you say, cousin Florence?"

"I said you were Reggie Wellington," said Florence simply.

"This Wellington I will not be," said George. "To be called after a boot!"

"What do boots matter!" Florence exclaimed. "Reggie is dark, like you. The aunts believed me, but Mr. Creed didn't."

"It was yesterday he saw me," said George. "He came

back for something—his tobacco pouch, I think. Our eyes met, and just then you called my name."

"Why didn't you say?" said Florence, vexed. "We could have thought of a story."

"I hoped perhaps he was poor-sighted. Or deaf," said George. "No matter—the story you made up is good. I shall be Reggie the boot, though I don't like it."

"I have a dreadful feeling that it's all coming to an end," said Florence. "The aunts say I should ask Reggie in."

"And that you can't do," George interrupted. "They would know me at once, that I am Georges. They would be dismayed."

"Oh—why?" Florence asked.

"They think that I am dead," said George.

"George—" Florence began.

"No. I don't answer you," said George. "If you ask such questions, I don't come anymore."

"Your English has all gone to pot," said Florence. "You really sound French today."

"My English is perfect," said George, insulted. "My mother is English—sister to your aunts. Four sisters—Cora, Dorothea, Jamesina, and Miriam. Cora is my mother; she is the pretty one."

"Are Dorrit and James really Dorothea and Jamesina?" said Florence. "I never knew. Miriam is my grandmother. She lives in China now."

"I know," said George. "Miriam is pretty, too. But not like my mother; my mother is beautiful."

Florence thought of her grandmother's thick white hair, which she herself loved to let down and brush and plait. "She was pretty once, I'm sure," she said. "I'm confused about ages, George, and dates—"

"Sh!" said George. "The Chancellor!"

But Mr. Creed was nowhere near.

4

Florence lay awake puzzling, that night. Should she invite the real Reggie to tea? It would help her deception with the aunts, but not with Mr. Creed. Mr. Creed might say at once that this was not the boy he had seen. If there was to be any plotting, she had to do it herself. George left it all to her. She finally decided to invite Reggie to tea on a Saturday, as soon as school began again.

And school was another problem. How could she go on seeing George next week, when school would fill her daylight hours, Monday to Friday? She even had prep. to do at home—spellings to learn, exercises to write—when she got back at 4:15. How would George like seeing her only in the evenings and at the weekends?

She soon had her answer. George didn't like it at all. He hated it that Florence never whistled to him immediately after her early breakfast—she was too occupied in getting, and staying, ready for school, her long hair wound into sausage curls, her boots shined, her dancing shoes in a drawstring bag, her books neat in her satchel. Sometimes he lurked in the bushes and put out his tongue at her when she got to the gate of the Paragon. He hated it too when Barbara or Winnie, Florence's nearest friends, called for her or walked home from school with her; their laughter on the pavement outside the Paragon gate—school jokes, girls' secrets—drove him wild. He rattled the bushes until Winnie backed away and said, "There's a dog in your garden, Florence," and Barbara, much afraid of dogs, ran away.

He hated Florence's staying in after tea to do her prep., and it was not long before there began to be interruptions to her work. If she worked in the kitchen, on the big scrubbed deal table, as she liked to do, she was safe; Mrs. Peabody or Hannah would be about. If she worked in the drawing room under the eye of the aunts she was also safe. But the dining room, where she might be sent if there was much cooking to be done and if the aunts were busy, was hopeless. George would somehow sniff out that she was there; fingers would drum on the windowpane and a face look out of the thicket of laurel leaves. The dining room had French doors and if these were unlatched George would come sliding in.

"Come on out, Florence," he would urge. "You've done enough." And Florence had no peace after that.

"Help me, first," she might say; but George was no scholar—except of course in French, which Florence had just begun, and in arithmetic, where he always knew the right answer, but seldom how to work the sum.

"I shall get awful reports this term," Florence grum-bled on one of these evenings.

"Who cares!" said George.

"Listen—there's somebody coming. Hide, George—under the table," Florence whispered.

"No," returned George, standing his ground. "You'll have to come out."

Florence had to—she was outside the French door, and George in the laurels, just in time. Her arithmetic went unfinished, and she got two out of ten for it next day.

The evenings were so long now, and so light, that there should have been ample time for George and Florence to meet; but the aunts had strong ideas about bedtime, and Florence's was half past eight, winter and summer alike. If she was still in the garden when half past eight struck, somebody would come out to call her. Florence was unusual among girls of that time in that she had a watch of her own, a present from the grandparents in China; it was a pretty thing, of blue enamel, and hung around her neck on a ribbon. She learned to be accurate in keeping to her bedtime—afraid that if she did not go in at once, a quick-eyed aunt would be out looking for her.

The day after the unfinished arithmetic, Florence had got out into the garden early, to try to keep the peace with George. At twenty past eight the two of them were near the top of the biggest apple tree, up to their chins in the pale pink flowers, giggling over the bending of supple branches under their feet.

"I'd better start down," said Florence regretfully.

"No!" exclaimed George with such violence that Florence shushed him automatically. But George would not stop. "You're always saying you've got to go. You wanted me, and I'm here. I wouldn't have come if you hadn't called for me. You've got to play with me now."

"But it's time—" said Florence, freeing one hand and reaching for her watch.

George leaned across from his branch and snatched the watch from her grasp; a quick jerk and the ribbon had broken, and George was off down the tree. Florence shouted at him, and followed as fast as she could; but when she reached the ground he had disappeared, and there was Aunt Dorrit coming around the end of the bank of lilac.

Florence burst into tears, which were not hard to explain. The lost watch—it had to be described as lost—was a tragedy the aunts could understand and share. Both aunts, and Hannah, helped Florence to search; but the watch was not to be found, and Florence went miserable to bed.

She woke with a start, in the darkness of her room, her heartbeat hammering and her spine prickling. Somebody was in the room. No, it was a voice—a voice at the window, calling "Florence!" low and hissingly.

Florence sat bolt upright, and stared at the dark. All the folk stories her father translated for her from his German book came flooding back to her. Goblins, witches who flew by night, ghosts who came out of churchyards and called the living by name . . . The local cemetery lay behind the house, only a short way away, acres it seemed of undulating land with graves—

George; it was only George. She recognized the voice now. Of course, it would be George.

"Let me in!" whispered George at the window.

Florence went across, but did not raise the heavy sash any higher.

"You must go away, George," she said. "It's the middle of the night. You'll wake people up."

"Come down, then," said George. "Look at the moon-light—it's just like day."

"I'd wake the aunts," objected Florence.

"But they both sleep in the front," said George. "Their bedrooms look over the street. They won't hear."

"Or Mrs. Peabody and Hannah," said Florence.

"Rubbish," said George. "They sleep in the basement; they'll never hear a thing. Come on, hurry up; if I let go of this wisteria I'll fall on the conservatory."

"What are you standing on?" said Florence.

"A little ledge in the brick," said George. "It's tiny. Are you coming, or do you want me to fall?"

"All right, all right," said Florence, the excitement of the new and daring driving the last of sleep from her. She pulled on her school clothes—the nearest to hand—and crept shoeless down the back stairs. Neither the back door nor the front door would open quietly, with their keys and chains and screechy bolts; but the French door in the dining room swung open with a whisper, and Florence was out on the grass. No sign of George: He must be at the back door. She stalked him through the laurels and pounced on him, suffocating with laughter; and the two shot away light-footed and silent into the bright, sharply shadowy kitchen garden and played their own kind of hopscotch over a pattern made on the path by laid-down garden stakes. George thought of game after game, and it was not until clouds covered the moon and the spring night grew cold that Florence could escape, creep back into the house, and shiver up the back stairs and into her chilly bed.

5

By now, George was doing all the summoning. This was the first night of many when he whistled below her window, or climbed up the ornamental ledges in the brick, holding by the wisteria branches. Florence half longed for George to come and half dreaded his coming. The warm nights of the spell of fine weather after Easter were one thing; but then came a stretch of frosty nights when Florence ached with cold and fatigue long before George tired of games; and after that a dark wet stretch—no moonlight, and heavy soaking showers.

"I'm not coming," said Florence into the rainy cavern of the night, her mouth to the crack of the French doors, which she just held apart.

"You must come," whispered George, half out of the laurel bushes.

"It's a beastly night and I want to go back to bed," Florence insisted.

"No!" said George violently. "What am I to do if you won't come out to play? You wanted me; it's your fault if you don't like it."

"I don't like it," said Florence wretchedly. "I want you to go away."

"Oh," said George. It was all he said, and he stood

dejected in the rain. Florence was overwhelmed with guilt.

"Can't I come in, then?" said George mournfully.

"How can you? We'd be heard," Florence answered.

"We can creep," said George. "There's the attic. That's miles from where anyone sleeps. Or the conservatory."

"Creep then," said Florence, and she let him in.

They did not dare to put on a light anywhere in the house, but padded from room to room and carefully, one step at a time, up the back stairs. Fortunately George remembered the Paragon—he seemed to know it as well as Florence did; but he complained once or twice, in an undertone, that the furniture was new or had been moved. In Aunt James's attic at last they felt safe, and dared to light one of the candles Aunt James kept there for emergencies—she had no faith in gaslight and had every expectation that it would either be cut off or explode.

There were two sections to the attic: huge rooms, each covering half the house. One half was used for storage and housed Aunt James's finished pictures, stacked against the wall; the other half was Aunt James's studio, where she painted close to a skylight. She also did much of her own framing, and her workbench was there.

George took the candle and peered critically at the canvases—lilies on one, against a background of clouds and water; Japanese anemones stiff and white on another; a tiny one of pansies.

"She doesn't get any better," he pronounced.

"Oh—don't you like them?" said Florence. "I do!" She

loved flowers, and Aunt James's accurate and pretty representations pleased her as they pleased hundreds of girls and women. She liked too the wide frames, sometimes of plush or velvet, that set the pictures off.

"They're not good art," said George. "You ask your father."

"What about Aunt Dorrit's?" said Florence. Aunt Dorrit painted portraits—always of women or children; she could somehow never manage men—or religious subjects. The religious subjects were always women or angels; ever since her picture of Moses had been described by Florence's father as "the bearded lady" she had given up trying to make her faces look masculine. All the same, the ladies who brought their daughters or little sons to Aunt Dorrit's studio went away pleased with the results.

"She's no better," said George. "Rather worse, perhaps, because she's more ambitious."

Florence thought this disloyal. "She's your *aunt*," she complained.

"Play something," said George.

"It will have to be quiet," said Florence.

The wet weather went on, and so did George's visits inside the house. Usually he and Florence went to the attic, but sometimes they visited the conservatory, where Aunt Dorrit had a wonderful arrangement of curtains to get the light right, and a red velvet sofa with a buttoned end for her sitters. She kept a few games there to entertain children who were allowed a break during sittings, and mercifully these included chess, draughts, backgammon, and cards. George's restlessness and preference for active games were always a nightmare to Florence inside the house, but these games were competitive enough to engross him, and chess in particular was a blessing. Her father had taught her to play in the long months when her mother was very ill, and she was a match for George. The two of them played for hours by candlelight in a tent of curtains.

After these wakeful nights Florence had to be shaken to get her to rouse at a quarter to eight in the morning, and she yawned her way through the day at school, "sadly inattentive" as her French teacher said. She was known to fall asleep in Scripture and once even in Nature Study, which she loved. She drooped over her cup and plate at teatime and the aunts and Mrs. Peabody began to watch her anxiously, alarmed by her pallor and the gray that showed between her cheekbones and her eyes.

Florence knew nothing of this, absorbed in keeping George quiet at night and planning new occupations. But messages passed between home and school; the aunts conferred frequently when she was in bed. Doctors were mentioned and an agreeable red tonic that tasted of iron was bought for Florence. The aunts kept Florence near them much more than usual, planned treats for her, invited Winnie and Barbara, Dick and Reggie to tea. She now saw George only at night, because of her aunts' vigilance; and even this, she felt, could not go on for long.

The aunts took to "looking in on" Florence when they went to bed themselves; they were early birds, so they always found Florence in bed and deeply asleep (George's visits were always after midnight now). Mrs. Peabody also took to looking in. She was early to bed as well; but she, unlike the aunts, was a bad sleeper and an occasional maker of cups of tea in the small hours. She was, if he had known it, George's worst enemy.

George had tired of chess and wanted to talk, that night, so Florence had said they must go up to the attic. Aunt James's workroom was at the back of the house, and much the safest place; and the two of them were there playing knucklebones.

"It's not a quiet game," Florence had objected.

"It's only noisy if you drop them. I don't drop them," said George—implying that Florence did. She did, too, and so in fact did he. It was this small sound, and not—fortunately—voices that Mrs. Peabody heard as she searched the house for Florence, having seen her empty bed.

"Sh! Listen!" said George suddenly.

Somebody was walking about on the floor below, where most of the bedrooms were; the door into one of the guest rooms shut with a click.

"George—we must hide!" whispered Florence. "Whoever it is, she'll come up. She must be looking for me."

"No—I'll hide," said George. "You must go down."

"But what shall I say?" said Florence.

"Don't say anything," said George.

When she saw Florence coming down the attic stairs Mrs. Peabody flattened herself against the wall to let Florence pass, and followed her without a word. Florence had decided that she should walk with dignity, not scuttle, and she passed Mrs. Peabody without a glance—simply staring ahead of her. She went straight to her room and got into bed. Mrs. Peabody, saying nothing, tucked her in and smoothed the hair off her forehead, and took and blew out the candle that Florence had carried down. Florence shut her eyes, puzzled but relieved, and pretended to sleep. She let half an hour go by before going back to the attic—to find no sign of George. Deciding he had gone, she went down and relocked the French door and returned to bed and to sleep.

6

It was Aunt Dorrit who woke Florence next morning, and she seemed unusually solicitous. "How do you feel, dear?" she asked.

"All right. A bit tired," said Florence, to account for a huge yawn.

"Well enough to go to school?" said Aunt Dorrit.

"Yes, of course," said Florence. "I'm not ill. Anyway I want to go. And I'm taking my hoop, Aunt Dorrit. We're going for a hoop run in the dinner hour. Miss Henson is taking us."

"A hoop run!" said Aunt Dorrit, staring at Florence's pale, exhausted face. "All right, Florence, you can get up."

Florence did badly in the hoop run, lagging behind the other girls of her class. Sometimes I used to be leader, she thought, as she fielded her runaway hoop from the side of the path. "Come on, Florence!" shouted Miss Henson, looking back. Florence's boots dragged and her knees ached.

"How did you get on in the hoop run?" asked Aunt James at tea.

Florence was surprised she should know about it. Why had Aunt Dorrit mentioned it to her?

"Not very well," she confessed. "I was a bit tired, I think."

"Now you're not to worry about this, Florence," said Aunt Dorrit. "But the reason you were a bit tired today was that you were walking in your sleep last night. People often do it, and your father used to when he was a boy. It doesn't matter, but don't be surprised if you wake up and find you're in the wrong room."

"Oh," said Florence. "How do you know? What happened?"

"Mrs. Peabody saw you," said Aunt James. "She didn't wake you, of course—just saw that you went safely back to bed."

"And we've got a piece of news for you," said Aunt Dorrit, brushing aside the subject of sleepwalking. "Your Uncle Crispin is coming to stay for a night."

"How lovely!" said Florence, remembering faintly a rosy laughing face and a loud, cheerful voice. "But he lives hundreds of miles away—almost in Scotland."

"Not anymore," said Aunt Dorrit. "I told you your Great-uncle Pearson had gone to live in the Isle of Wight on account of his health—well, Uncle Crispin and his family have moved to the old Pearson house, Bellfield in Sussex. It really isn't very far, so we shall see more of the Pearsons now. Do you remember your Pearson cousins?"

"Charles," said Florence. "And Isobel. They came here once. I've never seen the other children."

"Quite a tribe," said Aunt James. "Perhaps your uncle will bring their photographs."

"Perhaps," said Florence. She thought fleetingly of faded sepia and George with his challenging stare.

It was three more days before Uncle Crispin came: two nights with the problem of dealing with George. The first night, thundery and thickly dark, Florence refused to go out at all. She did not even open the French door, but undid the small window beside it, which had dark-blue plain glass mixed with panes with a reddish flower pattern, and leaned across a windowsill full of pots of fern to whisper.

"I'm not coming, George," she said. "I'm being watched—they think I walk in my sleep. It isn't safe. I'll come tomorrow." She shut the window fast before he could argue and hurried back to bed. George whistled under her window once or twice but, to her relief, he didn't climb the wisteria. Twice during the night she heard somebody open her door and saw the faint glimmer of a light from the landing outside.

The next night she went out as soon as her homework was finished, taking her hoop as an excuse. "I'm going out to practice," she called to Aunt Dorrit (in her conservatory, cleaning brushes) as she passed.

She had no need to whistle. George, in a fury of bad temper, met her around the corner of the lilacs.

"What do you mean, not coming, being watched!" he stormed—but in an undertone, like a cross conspirator. "I spent all the night by myself. It's too bad, Florence."

"I know, George; I can't help it," said Florence. "People keep looking in my room at night. I can't come tonight, either, so I've come to play with you now."

"Now and later," said George fiercely. Florence didn't comment but threw herself with fervor into a game of "he"—a wild game, with a touch of violence about it. When he caught her George did not touch, but grabbed; her evading him had a new reality about it.

Just before half past eight Florence led the game toward the house. She was running, George was chasing. She loitered for a moment and when he came up and reached to touch her she shot out a quick "Good-night," doubled around the lilacs, and was inside the conservatory door and bolting it behind her before he could decide what to do. Aunt Dorrit was still there, rubbing down an unsatisfactory beginning to a canvas.

"Is it bedtime, Aunt Dorrit?" Florence gasped.

"Good heavens, child, what have you been doing— you're cold as a marble saint, quite blue in the face with it," said Aunt Dorrit. "Get up to bed at once, and Mrs. Peabody will bring you a beaker of hot milk."

"Can I sleep in your room, or Aunt James's?" asked Florence, struck with an inspiration. "Then if I sleepwalk, you can stop me."

"Not at all a bad idea," said Aunt Dorrit. "You'd better go in with James; hers is much the bigger room. Go on and run your bath and I'll tell Mrs. Pea."

So if George climbed the wisteria that night, Florence never knew: tucked into the trundle bed in the corner of Aunt James's room, she slept unaware of anything, even Aunt James's "nervous tickle," which gave her coughing fits several times in the night.

37

Uncle Crispin Pearson was a doctor by profession, and to Florence's alarm it seemed to be more as a doctor than an uncle that he had come visiting. As soon as she got home from school he looked at her tongue and listened to her heart and asked her what seemed dozens of questions about food and sleep and lessons.

"So you enjoy your school?" he asked her finally, letting go of the wrist he had been holding.

"Most of it," said Florence. "Not dates of kings and battles, or capital cities of the world. We're doing algebra next year—I shall like that."

"And friends? You have lots of friends there?" he asked.

"Not dozens, but some," said Florence. "Winnie and Barbara, mostly. And Phyllis Flint. Have you brought any pictures of your children, Uncle Crispin?"

"Not this time," said Crispin. "Well! Suppose you have a wash and get ready for tea now. I'll tell you about your cousins over tea."

Florence obediently went, but the door did not quite shut behind her, and her ear went at once to the crack.

"Nothing too wrong that I can see," Uncle Crispin was saying. "It's more in the mind than the body, I should suppose. Does she miss her father much?"

Florence could not distinguish the reply.

"Yes, well, and she'll be grieving for her mother still," came Uncle Crispin's voice.

"But that's almost two years—" Aunt James began.

"Time's of little significance," said Uncle Crispin. "Grief's a funny thing. You should know that, James."

"The point is, do we send for her father?" Aunt Dorrit asked. "He said he'd come at once if there was anything, but these frescoes he's found are quite unknown and he thinks they're important; and there's another man with an interest in them hovering around."

"Not necessary, I should say," said Uncle Crispin. "What I thought was—" He lowered his voice so that the next part was hard to catch, but Florence made out a phrase or two: "country air," "house full of children," "racket around a bit." She tiptoed off and got herself washed and brushed for tea.

It was hard to seem entirely surprised when Uncle Crispin said at tea, "The aunts and I think you need a holiday, Florence my dear, so I'm plotting to take you off with me tomorrow and let you get to know all your cousins firsthand—now what do you say to that? A big house with a garden and fields all around it, no end of space, six children all ages (six when I last counted, anyway), food straight from the farms, and the downs for climbing—what do you say to it, eh?"

"But what about school? There's a lot more term to go," said Florence.

"What's a few weeks here or there? You can read our Nellie's books—she's nearest to your age—and lessons won't spoil for being left a bit," said Uncle Crispin. "Now would you like to come, or not?"

"Yes, please," said Florence. She smiled at Uncle Crispin and put out of her head, most firmly, all thoughts of a moonlit garden and a Call Song and her other "cousin," whom nobody would talk about at all.

PART TWO

Late May to Mid-December 1910
at Bellfield

1

The flurry of packing and planning filled the rest of the day, and it was not until Florence was tucked into the trundle bed in Aunt James's room that she really remembered George. She sat up in bed, thinking how mean it would be not to say good-bye, not to tell him anything before she went; but the dread of the scene there would undoubtedly be overcame her and she ducked under the bedclothes again. All the same, before she got dressed next morning she slipped into the small trunk ready for her journey a handkerchief-wrapped parcel that contained a photograph and a penknife.

The aunts kissed and hugged Florence and wished her a good journey and happy holidays, and Mrs. Peabody and Hannah shook her hand. The cab taking her and Uncle Crispin to the station drove away from the Paragon with no sign of anybody else, in the garden trees or the shrubbery; and Florence uncrossed her fingers and sighed with relief.

"Cheer up," said Uncle Crispin. "You'll love Bellfield. Everybody does."

Uncle Crispin's descriptions of Bellfield were vague, and Florence hoped to get a better picture out of him on the journey; but the journey was so full of its own delights that they talked about nothing but these. Florence loved trains, soot and all. And at Midhurst Station Aunt Addy was waiting to drive them to Bellfield in the trap.

"Thought I'd come myself," she said in her usual hurried and energetic way. "The children fought like cats as to who should come too, so I left the lot of them behind. Come along, Florence, room for you by me. D'you want to learn to drive? I'll teach you, but we won't start today. Or Isobel will. She's quite a good little whip. Mind your feet, now. There's a dog in here somewhere."

Florence was glad she had been warned, as the dog licked her knees in the gap between her skirt and her long socks. She tried to look at the countryside, but had hardly a chance to take in anything—so rapid was Aunt Addy's conversation—except that the village was not set in the prairie that Uncle Crispin's references to fields and open air had suggested. It was rather a land of gentle valleys, rounded hilltops, patches of heathery common, and clumps and clusters of rich-growing trees. As for the house itself, she got only the impression of something high and gray and full of white-shuttered windows before what seemed a horde of children surrounded the trap and a groom was there to take the reins. Two effervescent small boys boarded the trap to hug their father.

"Out, you young Turks!" shouted Uncle Crispin good-humoredly above the din. "And help your cousin down. Mind the step, Florence."

"I shall never know them all," said Florence, taking fright at the number of young faces around.

"Know them by tomorrow," said Uncle Crispin, jumping down from the trap. "Charles isn't here, for a start—

he's a weekly boarder at his school. So the young ones are pining—aren't you, Ferdy? Aren't you, Marc?" Ferdinand and Marcus, two skinny, mouse-haired boys, giggled and scuffled their feet in the gravel, staring at Florence with concentration.

"And here's the eldest of the girls, my Isobel," said Uncle Crispin, hugging a pretty, rosy-faced thirteen-year-old. "And Audrey's the youngest, aren't you, kitten? And so, very special. Who's missing? Where's Nellie got to?"

One girl, dark and straight-haired, hung back from the group, watching intently.

"Come along, Nell!" called Aunt Addy, and the girl came forward reluctantly. Florence wondered if she was shy and looked at her with special interest. Nellie didn't smile but looked at her expressionlessly.

Audrey, who clearly had no problem of shyness, grasped Florence's hand and dragged her up the three steps and in at the front door.

"I'll show you where you're sleeping," she said. "Mr. Rich will bring in your box. Then I'll show you my dollhouse. Then we'll have tea." Life seemed a simple matter for Audrey; if she wanted something, it happened.

"Don't let her wear you out, Florence," said Aunt Addy, coming into the house behind them.

Florence was quite pleased to be taken over and shown around by the commanding Audrey.

"This is your room," said Audrey, opening a door into a white room with blue flowers on the wallpaper and a blue-and-white patchwork quilt on the bed. "It's Nellie's really, but she's sharing with me while you're here. Mummy thought you'd like a room to yourself."

Florence said nothing, but wished it had not been the grave-faced Nellie who had been moved out for her sake.

"We've only been here six months, and not all the rooms are finished yet," said Audrey. "We haven't begun on the attics. When we do there'll be a bedroom for each of us, and a proper playroom. Now here's my dollhouse. Look, all the front opens out and you can see the rooms. I'll let you play with it, if you like."

"Do Isobel and Nellie play with it?" asked Florence.

"Not anymore," said Audrey. "Isobel's nearly grownup now, and puts on airs. I don't know what Nellie does."

Audrey turned out to be a blessing to Florence in her first days at Bellfield. Isobel, far from putting on airs, was friendly and fun. She thought Florence, whom she described as "half an orphan," romantic and interesting, and did her many small kindnesses. She loved putting Florence's hair into curls and was handy at mending falling hems and loose collars (Aunt Addy was hopeless with a needle). She gave Florence a ring too small for her own fingers, and a pair of her outgrown slippers, which Florence passionately loved—ivory silk, with pink roses on the toes. She made sure Florence understood all the family games. But she was burdened with homework, and busy with many other things—the watering of all the indoor plants, and the geraniums in pots around all the windows, was Isobel's job because her mother never remembered such things. Nellie remained silent and withdrawn, reading in much of her spare time or writing an interminable diary that nobody was allowed to see. Ferdy and Marcus careered about together, bound up in their own secrets and their own ploys. Audrey always had time for Florence and was only too glad of a willing audience or storyteller.

"You watch out, Cousin Florence," said Charles on his first weekend visit home after Florence's arrival. "Audrey can be a proper little tyrant. There's nothing she likes better than a slave."

"No I don't, then, Charlie," said Audrey. "I don't have slaves, I have very special friends. Florence is my friend. I'm your best friend here, aren't I, Florence?"

"I don't know, Audrey," said Florence. (Nellie, blank-faced as ever, looked up from her book.) "How can I say, when everybody here is so nice?" (Nellie smiled faintly— but not at Florence—and looked down again.)

"First prize for tact goes to Florence," said Charlie, laughing. "Come on, Queen Audrey, let's all play charades. You too, Nellie. You can take your nose out of Walter Scott for once."

"It isn't Walter Scott," said Nellie, self-possessed as usual. "It's *Cranford*." But she shut the book and joined in the charades with a sparkle Florence had never seen her show before. Indeed, the whole family had an extra liveliness when Charles was at home: Games were wilder, conversations funnier; even the grown-ups seemed somehow wider awake.

Florence was disappointed to find that she was not going to school with the girls. Isobel, Nellie, and Audrey were driven off every morning in the trap to their school in

Midhurst; Ferdy and Marcus, whose school was nearer, went off on bicycles, chattering and calling.

"Couldn't I go, too?" she asked Aunt Addy. "I'd be in Nellie's class. I'd fit in, I know I would."

Nellie's face was stony.

"You need a little rest, Florence," said Aunt Addy. "Your great-aunts, and your Uncle Crispin, all think you ought to have a break from school. You can sit with me—we'll have some French conversation, and we'll read together. Wave them good-bye and come and help me decide what we'll have to eat today."

Within a few days, Florence found that she was belonging with no effort—and no boredom, either. Most of the mornings she spent with Aunt Addy, helping with household matters. Mrs. Rich, the housekeeper, developed a soft spot for Florence and taught her how to make bread, and raisin cakes, and lemon curd; and how to sew.

"It won't have escaped your notice, madam," said Mrs. Rich to Aunt Addy, "that having lost her mother so young, and the poor lady ill a long time beforehand, Miss Florence can hardly sew a seam."

"You know I don't notice such things, Mrs. Rich," said Aunt Addy, "being no use at all myself. Were you thinking you might have a moment to show her, now?"

"You don't need to bother, Mrs. Rich," said Florence anxiously. "They'll teach me at school, but we haven't got far yet. I can do buttonholes."

"Buttonholes!" said Mrs. Rich. "There's no joy in buttonholes." Florence was puzzled, until she discovered that Mrs. Rich's idea of sewing was not mending sheets and patching torn petticoats, but smocking and gathers and frills and embroidery with fine silk. Florence loved this, and spent an hour most mornings in Mrs. Rich's sitting room with a grandfather clock ticking lazily, and her feet on a buttoned stool for comfort as she sat in Mrs. Rich's high armchair. The gossip of the servants, as they came for instructions, went on all around her and Mrs. Rich fed her on buttermilk and cherry cake.

Occasionally, Florence went out with Uncle Crispin on his rounds; but he didn't much like to leave her alone outside the houses where he had ill people to visit, though she was prepared to stay in the trap holding the reins, and the horse stood quietly for her—even when one of the noisy newfangled motorcars came by. People were always asking her in, and he didn't approve of her going into houses where there was illness. More often she went out calling, with Aunt Addy, in the afternoons; Aunt Addy had friends in many neighboring villages and in Midhurst, and some of them were quite pleased to have a new person to entertain. There were some houses where Aunt Addy thought Florence would be bored, and on these days Florence stayed at home. She enjoyed it, too, when Aunt Addy had afternoon guests herself; Florence got skillful at handing around tea and cakes and curtsying politely. Often the grown-ups' conversation was interesting; if it wasn't she played with Adolphus, Aunt Addy's little spaniel, or drew in the thick book that she called her sketchbook. Some visitors liked her to draw them and one or two even asked to have the pictures to keep. Florence's drawings weren't at all bad.

Aunt Addy's intention of seeing that Florence kept up

her schoolwork rather faded out; but she did talk French to Florence and encourage her to reply. Florence fumbled and stumbled and wished she had made George teach her a bit.

It was not often that she thought of George. Sometimes she remembered uncomfortably her common sense (or was it cowardice? How could you tell?) in leaving London without a word to him. But part of her new ease at Bellfield was the absence of a worry and a secret. No George, no concealment: Florence was just a schoolgirl staying with her cousins. She grew relaxed and contented; her thin cheeks filled out a little and her knees and elbows stuck out a little less. She wrote regularly to the aunts, as she did to her father, but London seemed as far away as Italy, and she was glad.

"Are you happy, Florence?" Aunt Addy asked her once when they had come back wet from one of their outings and were drying their skirts by a fire Mrs. Rich had lit for them.

"Yes, I am, Aunt Addy," said Florence. "Bellfield's like another home, now, and I love it. There's one thing, though." She paused.

"Well?" prompted Aunt Addy.

"Nellie doesn't like me," said Florence, feeling uncomfortable.

"You don't want to worry about Nellie," said Aunt Addy. "Leave her alone and give her time. She hasn't made up her mind about you yet. She's a passionate soul, and if she decides to like you she'll like you forever."

"I thought perhaps she didn't want an extra person in the family," said Florence. "You know, pushing in."

"I don't think it's jealousy," said Aunt Addy. "But wait and see."

"She's not like the others, is she?" said Florence. "She's so quiet. And so dark."

"She takes after my side of the family, not your uncle's," said Aunt Addy. "Except that she's better-looking than I am. Oh yes"—seeing Florence look surprised—"Nellie's going to be the beauty of the family. Fortunately she doesn't know it yet, so you'd better not mention it."

"I wish I wasn't dark," said Florence, who preferred Isobel and Audrey's light-brown curls to Nellie's grave looks. "I suppose I take after my mother: She was dark like the aunts."

"You've got the Gage looks," said Aunt Addy. "Of course, the person you really resemble is Georges Valery."

Florence drew in too large a gulp of air. "But how do you know George?" she said.

"Did—he's dead," said Aunt Addy. "I'm a Gage too, you know. I spent a lot of time with the aunts, when I was a girl, and I knew all the family."

"George was half French, wasn't he?" said Florence.

"Half French, but both halves dark," said Aunt Addy. "Still—we aren't talking about George."

"Nobody does," said Florence, vexed at seeing a possible way into the subject closing up. "I'd like to know about him."

"You must ask your father, when he comes home," said Aunt Addy. "He knows more of the story than anybody else."

So there is a story, thought Florence.

2

The few afternoons when she was left at home, when
her uncle and her aunt were out, were at first difficult
for Florence; but she soon discovered a whole world of
things to do. Some of Nellie's books had been left in her
bedroom and on wet days she read these with a variety
of reactions; her favorites were *Hiawatha* and a book
called *English Ballads*. She especially liked the ballads
with ghosts and demons in them, like "The Demon
Lover," and the ones with stories of brave and resource-
ful girls, like "The Outlandish Knight." On fine days she
usually escaped from the garden—a rather formal one
and not nearly so large as the aunts' in London—into
her uncle's orchard, where there were long grass and
climbable trees; or the paddock near the house; or the
meadow beyond that.

When Uncle Crispin was driving the brown cob,
Charlie (called Charlie-horse to distinguish him from
Charlie-boy, Florence's cousin), and Aunt Addy was driving the black mare, Dinah, there was one horse left in
the paddock—Dolly, an old gray who was in retirement
partly through old age and partly through extreme lazi-
ness, which made driving her a struggle. Florence decided, without telling anyone, that she would learn to ride

Dolly. She was not sure where to find, or how to put on, Dolly's saddle, so she threw an old rug from the summer-house over Dolly and climbed up with the help of the meadow gate. Dolly always wore a headstall, but there was of course no bit to this. Florence looped the halter and knotted it to the far side of the headstall as if it were reins, kicked Dolly, and hoped for the best. At first Dolly would only walk a few steps and go back to feeding, but after a while she suddenly woke up and broke into a trot. Florence fell off at once, but was not discouraged and mounted again. She went back on several afternoons, taking an empty toy box to act as a mounting block, and rode Dolly with increasing success. As she always went with her pinafore pockets full of apples or carrots, begged from Mrs. Rich, Dolly came to regard her as a friend and would even, in short bursts, canter for her. Florence had no idea why she kept these times with Dolly a secret. Audrey said to her once, "Where've you been? You smell of horse," and Florence said truthfully, "Feeding old Dolly. It's nice with her in the paddock," and Audrey commented, uninterested, "Oh—Dolly! I wish we could all have Arab steeds that would gallop."

"Girls don't gallop," said Marcus, who was temporarily separated from Ferdy and watching proceedings in the dollhouse.

"Yes they do," said Audrey. "Isobel can ride Charlie-horse and when she's older she wants to ride to hounds."

"Fat chance," said Marcus. "Doctors' daughters don't ride to hounds."

"Neither do doctors' sons, then," said Audrey.

"Doctors' sons don't want to," said Marcus. "Doctors' sons go to sea and are admirals when they grow up."

One hot afternoon in early June, when the other children were all at school, Florence went on one of her riding expeditions. Dolly was especially sleepy and the paddock, ringed by its great elm trees, seemed enchanted by sun and silence. Dolly and Florence ambled several times around; Florence had little power of steerage except her heels, and Dolly went more or less where she liked. Stung by one of the summer flies, Dolly suddenly broke into a canter and went charging down the side of the field, close under the line of elms. Florence hung on to Dolly's tough mane and looked up to make sure that no low elm branches would hit her in the face. Sitting among the branches of the tree she was approaching, and looking down toward her through the leaves, was a boy, staring at her, dark-eyed. It was George.

A branch she had forgotten, in her shock, to duck underneath caught Florence across the chest and she was swept off Dolly's back and to the ground.

It was teatime before she was missed, with Aunt Addy back from her trip to Midhurst, the children back from school, and Uncle Crispin changing his boots after his afternoon calls. (Aunt Addy always made him change them when he got in—as if his patients had foot-and-mouth disease and he might carry infection home.) Florence was called in the house and the garden, and the boys shouted for her over the orchard fence: no results.

"She sometimes goes to feed Dolly," offered Audrey, just as people were beginning to feel anxious.

"The paddock!" said Isobel. "I'll go." Ferdy accompanied her, and got there first; he was swinging on the gate when she arrived.

"Nobody here," he said, surveying the untroubled expanse of grass and thistles.

"Why has Dolly got a blanket on, in this heat?" said Isobel. "Ferdy—her shadow's a funny shape."

Dolly was standing over Florence where she lay stunned in the grass, and so Isobel had all the glory of finding her. Ever practical, Isobel sent Ferdy racing to the house, covered Florence with Dolly's blanket, and waved the flies away with a dock leaf until Uncle Crispin (in the wrong shoes) came running.

Florence woke in bed, physically well and comfortable; and she woke in no confused state but knowing instantly what had happened. She had seen George. George was at Bellfield.

"I'm all right," she said to Aunt Addy, who was sitting by her bed. "I've got all my arms and legs. I didn't break anything."

Uncle Crispin came from the other side of the room. "Yes, you're not damaged," he said. "What happened? Can you remember?"

Florence had a moment's wild impulse to say, "I saw Georges Valery sitting in an elm tree," but restrained it. "I fell off Dolly," she said.

"Were you riding Dolly?" said Aunt Addy. "My dear

girl, you should have had her saddle on her. No wonder you fell off."

"I often ride her, with just a blanket on," said Florence. "She's all right. A branch knocked me down, I think. Something startled her and she went off at top speed, all at once."

"Gadfly, most likely," said Uncle Crispin. "It happens at this time of year. Now does your head ache? Does it hurt here?"

"It doesn't hurt anywhere," said Florence. "Why am I in bed?"

"To be on the safe side," said Uncle Crispin. "You did knock yourself out. Have the evening in bed and get up tomorrow."

As soon as her aunt and uncle had gone—Aunt Addy to fetch her thin bread and butter and a cup of tea—Florence slid out of bed and went to look out of the window. She was afraid of seeing a dark boy in the garden. But the rose and delphinium beds looked peaceful; there was a wholesome smell of pinks; and nobody lurked among the limes along the garden's edge.

3

Florence was treated as convalescent for two days, only allowed up for a part of each day and given invalid's food: bread-and-milk, which she loved, and beef tea, which she thought revolting. Isobel came up conscientiously while Florence was in bed, to bring books and little pots of flowers and to read to her. Ferdy and Marcus put their heads around the door and told her jokes or recited funny verses. Audrey came with the dollhouse dolls to play with them on Florence's bed. Nellie came once, a duty visit.

"Mummy said I should come—that it wasn't polite not to," she said, standing with her hands clasped behind her, just inside the door.

"Oh," said Florence. "I've been reading your book about King Arthur. And the book of ballads with 'The Outlandish Knight' in it. I hope you don't mind."

"'He told me he'd take me to that northern land,/And there he would marry me'," said Nellie (and Florence was relieved to realize she was only quoting). "What really happened in the paddock?"

"What I said," said Florence, suddenly nervous. "I fell off Dolly."

"Why were you riding her?" asked Nellie.

"Can't I?" said Florence. "Aunt Addy only said I ought to have a saddle."

"She belongs to Daddy," said Nellie.

"I'll ask him, then," said Florence, and Nellie went away.

Florence was glad to have a two-day interval before going anywhere on her own. She was worried and afraid of how George would next appear, and who would see him. She thought about him a good deal and all her thoughts were dark ones. How had he tracked her to Bellfield? He had no business to. He was not meant to come here: He would make life too difficult. How could she deal with him in a house as full as Bellfield, when even in the quiet of the Paragon he had been seen by Mr. Creed? She did not think he would dare to come indoors at Bellfield—but there was always just the possibility that he would simply ring the front-door bell and come in and say "I'm your kinsman Georges Valery—how do you do?" She looked apprehensively out of every window she passed and into all the corners of any room she entered.

The third day she was pronounced better and told she could do what she liked, but was not to tire herself. It was a Saturday, and by midmorning Charles came home from his school, fetched by Aunt Addy in the trap; welcomed, as usual, by all the children capering and singing "Charlie is My Darling" on the front steps. Isobel hugged him ecstatically.

"Mind my cake, Bel," he said, holding above his head a white confectioner's box. "I made Ma stop at the baker's—I had some pocket money left. We'll have a feast. Somebody fetch a knife and somebody beg some lemonade from the kitchen. Florence, are you better? I heard you were doing circus tricks on old Dolly. Madame la Flo, daring bareback rider! Good for you."

Florence giggled. "I've got a knife," she said. "I'll get it."

"Oh good," said Charles. "Pa confiscated all our penknives because we were practicing throwing them and Audrey's ear got cut. Silly, really—it wasn't much of a cut."

"It was, Charlie—it bled all down my neck and on my dress and petticoat," said Audrey.

All the Pearson children went off to hunt for lemonade, and Florence ran up to her room—which she still thought of as Nellie's room—to look for George's knife.

She had some difficulty in finding it. She knew that both the knife and photograph were in a blue leather writing case that her father had given her. Her father had bought it in the city of Florence and had written on a card inside, "Florence, from Florence," and drawn a picture of a violet. Florence loved the soft leather and the fleur-de-lis pattern stamped into it in gold. She had hidden the knife among her pens and the photograph among her envelopes. The photograph seemed to be still in place—though hadn't she left the flap of the envelope that contained it tucked in?—but the knife was nowhere to be seen.

A shout came up the stairs from Charles, "Come on, Florence! We're ready for the feast," and Florence tried to hurry. She looked in the drawer where the writing case had been, and finally found the knife loose at the bottom of the drawer, its blade open—and surely she had left it shut? With no time for speculation Florence ran headlong down the stairs.

The cake was cut and eaten in the bamboo summer-house on the boundary between the garden and the orchard, and washed down with lemonade drunk from a jug that passed from hand to hand.

"Nice knife, Madame la Flo," said Charles, who had done the cutting. "Why does it say G.V. on the handle?"

"Is it a mystery?" said Marcus hopefully as Florence hesitated, and Nellie's eyes turned to her, watchful.

"No—it's my father's knife, that's all," said Florence. "He must have got it from a friend."

"His boyhood companion, drowned at sea—" began Audrey.

"No, no, not at sea, or the knife would have gone down with him," said Nellie unexpectedly. "Found in his pocket when they dragged the river."

"Ghouls!" said Charles. "Put it somewhere safe, Florence; it's silver. Leave your pinafores, girls—they show up like beacons—and let's all get out of our boots. We're going to play lion hunt."

"Will it be dry enough in the meadow?" said Isobel. "There was a shower yesterday."

"Sucks to the shower," said Ferdy. "The hay will be cut soon, and the game's no good when the grass is short. We must play today."

Boots, socks, and pinafores were abandoned in the summerhouse and George's knife tucked inside one of Florence's boots. Florence followed the others to the meadow with some trepidation. She would have felt happier with something on her feet. And what was lion hunt?

The meadow, a big field beyond orchard and paddock, stood like a sea of grass tossing slightly in the sunny breeze. The grass was almost up to Florence's waist, reddish and shiny with seed and glowing with the extra color of buttercups and sorrel. Lion hunt needed a lot of space as well as really long grass. Charles insisted on being the first lion; the others all chose the name of an animal that might be the lion's prey. (Florence got in quickly with antelope; Audrey, slow off the mark, got left with goat.) The various animals crawled on all fours through the long grass trying to avoid the lion; if they met they were allowed to consult one another as to his whereabouts. The game went on until the lion got a victim. When he was close to one, he was obliged to let out a roar before he pounced; the victim was then allowed to run for the hedge and if he or she got there first the game began again. If the lion—now also allowed to run—made a kill, the victim had to be lion next.

Florence had no wish to be lion, so she kept fairly close to the hedge and got quite pink in the face from holding her breath and listening for the movement of other animals. The meadow was very quiet, apart from the rustle and hiss of the grass, and a few larks high up sounded close and clear. Florence once saw a gleam of light brown between the grass stalks—Isobel or Audrey, who both had brown dresses. She crawled closer and met Isobel face to face. "Where feeds the king of beasts, O antelope?" whispered Isobel, following the correct formula.

"I know not, O eland; not set eyes on him," Florence whispered back.

"He fed in the far north when I got wind of him last—over near the big tree," answered Isobel. "Go carefully, sister antelope!" And she crawled away, stifling a laugh.

Florence began to get bored with hugging the hedge, and found too some nettly patches there, which were hard on hands and knees. She decided to be wildly adventurous and head for the center of the field. On the way there, skirting a mighty clump of thistles, she saw a dark-blue patch between the grass and thistle leaves, and a shine of dark hair above it. That meant Nellie. What would happen, she wondered, if she met Nellie close to in the long grass, on all fours, and simply said, "Let's be friends. I never wanted to be an intruder. I'm sorry I've got your room"? She parted the grass ahead of her and whispered "Zebu!" which was Nellie's beast. The other animal parted its own grass, turning toward her; and she found herself staring at George. Florence drew in so sharp a breath that she felt that the lion must hear her, half the field away.

George grinned. "Meet the bushbuck," he said. "You didn't know I was playing."

"I didn't know you were here—until I fell off Dolly," said Florence.

"You didn't have to fall off," said George.

Florence watched him, wondering what to say. He looked, she thought, somehow different from the George of London. More serious, was it? Sadder? More intense?

"You must go away," she said.

"Oh?" said George. His eyebrows drew together, and

his mouth turned grim. "Now you're telling me to go away—but it was you who fetched me."

"I didn't fetch you here," said Florence. "I won't meet you and play with you here."

"Playing doesn't matter," said George. "But you must meet me, Florence, and you will. Meet me here tonight, when everyone's asleep. If you don't promise now this minute, I'll stand straight up and shout, 'Look at me everybody! I'm George.'"

"All right," said Florence hurriedly. "I'll come."

Charles suddenly roared, not many feet away; and there was a thudding of feet and the squeals of Ferdy (the gnu) as he ran for the hedge. Florence leaped to her feet to watch the chase; when she looked back, Ferdy having been noisily caught, George had gone.

Although the game went on until the grass was flattened (Florence was lion once herself, and caught Isobel) there was never a chance to come face to face with Nellie and whisper "Let's be friends."

4

Florence could not conceal from herself that she was afraid of going by night to meet George. The smaller house in London, which she knew so well, and its familiar garden, were one thing; the echoing darkness of the downstairs of Bellfield at night, and the huge spaces of garden and orchard, paddock and meadow, held a new terror. During the rest of the lion hunt Saturday she crept about the house, thinking of ways and means, laying plans.

She didn't know the ways of Bellfield as she did those of the Paragon. Did Uncle Crispin sit up late, and if so, in which room? Which door did night callers wanting a doctor come to? And which doors were locked at night, and who had keys? She had no idea of these things.

But she knew what to look for. An unimportant door onto the garden, or a convenient window; and a dark lantern she could use to navigate the stretch of garden before the meadow if the moon wasn't adequate to light her around flower beds and shrubs. Aunt Addy was a great rose lover and Florence shrank from the thought of an encounter with fierce triangular thorns or cascading showers of hooky twigs.

By evening she had her plan of action. The most

secluded door was a small garden door in the passage between the library and the patients' waiting room; patients often left by this door to avoid having to be shown out at the front. It had stiff bolts top and bottom but it didn't, as far as Florence could recollect, have a key—there was a keyhole, but Mr. Rich never locked the door when he did his evening rounds, only shot the bolts. There was also a borrowable dark lantern in Uncle Crispin's cloakroom beside his surgery, where he washed his hands and changed his boots when he came in from visiting.

By evening she had also acquired a tense, drawn look.

"What's the matter, Flo? Are you seeing things?" asked Charles casually as the children ate supper.

Aunt Addy, who was sitting with them, glanced at Florence sharply.

"You look tired out, Florence," she said. "Straight to bed for you. Yes, you can go now, if you've finished."

Thankful, Florence escaped upstairs. Although nobody looked in on her at night here, she really did go to bed, and even to sleep. Maybe, she thought as she buried her face in the pillow, she wouldn't wake till morning; nothing would happen.

There was nothing to climb around Florence's window at Bellfield—no wisteria, not even a drainpipe. Her side of the house stood stark and bare, above the level where a climbing rose bore huge moonlike blooms. Florence had shut her window and she never knew what woke her. Not a voice, not a whistled tune. But she did wake, in still darkness, stifling hot, to the unhappy recollection of a promise. She had said to George, "All right, I'll come"; and however little she might want to go, her promise stood.

In the dark, she put on her warm dressing gown and knee-length socks, and she picked up her boots in her hand. Not getting properly dressed seemed a sign that she wasn't going out for long—half going, not going properly. This seemed clear to her but she wasn't certain it would be so clear to George.

It was all very well, she now realized, to know where her uncle's lantern was; she had to get there without putting on lights in the sleeping house. She crept very slowly, feeling for walls, clutching at banisters, glad of the gleam of a night-light from Nellie and Audrey's room and of the stray beams coming in from the outdoor lamp that shone over the front door to light any people coming late and urgently for a doctor. She got herself downstairs and to her uncle's cloakroom, and found his lantern and the matches for the candle inside it. Once it was lit she felt altogether happier; and happier still once the bolts of the garden door had slid open without grinding and she had got the door shut behind her without a bang. She sat on the step outside and put on her boots by feel, and was off over the dark grass.

It was not until she was some way from the house that she dared to open the lantern shutter; after that she made better speed. She had forgotten how wet the garden would be after a fine day and heavy dew; water soon clogged the long skirts of her dressing gown, and the branches that touched her as she crossed from grass patch to grass patch swept over her head with wet fronds.

When she reached the end of the paddock she put the lantern down, and sat on the gate between paddock and meadow, staring into the darkness. There was light from a newish moon, but very little. The meadow and paddock seemed empty—or almost empty. A black shape and a heavy noise of breathing, coming toward her from the paddock side of the gate, was Dolly—or was it one of the other horses? Florence balanced on the gate, listening and trying to see. It couldn't be Dolly; it was too tall. It was too tall for Dinah, even, or Charlie-horse. It must be a monster—a tall, horselike monster—

Florence gripped the gate on either side of her, too frightened to move.

"It's only Dolly," said George's voice from the top part of the monster. "And me on her. What did you think it was—a nightmare?"

Florence didn't say anything. She was too busy getting her breath back after holding it for so long.

"Or is it I who am the nightmare, as far as you're concerned?" George went on, his voice bitter. "You show it clear enough that you don't want me."

"I said I didn't want you here," said Florence feebly. "You don't belong here, George. How can you be a secret here, with a house full of people, and all the other children watching me?"

"That's why you don't want me, isn't it?" said George. "All the other children. The nice new cousins. I was your cousin first, Florence. Before you ever knew them, I came when you called."

"I know," said Florence. "But it won't work here, George. It never could. People will see me coming and going, and they'll put extra locks on the doors, and someone will be put in my room to watch me in the night."

"So you have a room to yourself," said George. "That's useful."

"But people watch me," said Florence. "It's not like the Paragon, the two old aunts and the servants in the basement. There are bedrooms all around."

"You wouldn't say any of this if you wanted me," said George. "If you wanted me, you'd find out ways. But you don't. Do you, Florence?"

"No," whispered Florence. "Not really. Not here. I told you. It's different here."

"School holidays are almost here," said George. "Perhaps they'll go away. You'll be left with the servants. You'll want me then."

"They'd take me with them," said Florence. "I wouldn't be left alone."

"Which one do you like best?" said George, sounding suddenly fierce. "Is it Charlie?"

"No," said Florence. "Audrey, I think. But it might be Nellie, if she'd talk to me."

"Nellie," said George. "That's one better than Charlie, anyway. If it were Charlie, I'd—"

He stopped and drew a jerky breath.

"George, you're not crying, are you?" said Florence. "I don't want that. I don't want you miserable."

"Naturally I'm not crying," said George. "Do you think I'd cry for you? Don't drive me away, that's all."

Florence said nothing. She seemed to have run out of arguments; and George saw his advantage at once.

"You can come out here again," he said, almost wheedling. "You came tonight, and nobody saw you. You can do it again."

"No, I can't," said Florence, her fingers, which had loosened, gripping the gate again. "I can't, George. I won't."

"Just once, then," said George. "I can't make you keep on coming. But just once. Tomorrow. Come tomorrow night."

"All right, just once," said Florence. "Just tomorrow."

"It's a promise," said George. "And now, we'll ride."

He edged Dolly close to the gate, and with a strength Florence did not realize he had—the strength, it seemed, of a grown man—he hauled her up onto the horse in front of him.

"Hold her mane," he shouted in Florence's ear, drowning her protests. Florence bunched up her dressing-gown skirts as best she could (she couldn't dismount, as George held her firmly around the waist) and took Dolly's mane in both hands. George drove his heels into Dolly's sides and Dolly, with a snort, kicked up her heels and went off down the paddock at a rapidly accelerating trot, at a canter, at—was this a gallop? Florence had never supposed Dolly could gallop, certainly not with two people on her back; but this was a faster pace than she had ever experienced. George rested his chin on her shoulder, laughing close to her ear. Florence, afraid of the headlong speed in the dark (Could Dolly see where she was going? Would they hit the hedge and land head-first in the hawthorn?), shouted to him to stop.

"Why stop?" George shouted back. "It's a dream—it's magic. Get on, Dolly!"

Florence didn't know how many times they circled the paddock; she became exhausted as well as frightened, and wondered whether George would ever get tired too and if not, how they would stop. Dolly settled the matter. She stopped of her own accord, near the gate, abruptly; and Florence and George were thrown off over her neck. They fell soft, in the swathes of wet grass, George still laughing; and Dolly disappeared into the darkness, panting and snorting heavily. Florence hit George hard in the chest with her right fist, but George didn't much care.

"Don't say you didn't enjoy it," he said. "Don't say you don't have fun and adventure when I'm here."

"I was scared stiff," said Florence. "You're hateful. And I won't come tomorrow."

"Yes, you will," said George. "You promised. And you'll come."

"I hate you," said Florence, and ran for the gate and the house.

The lantern was easy to find, beside the gate, but the candle inside it had burned down and out and Florence had to feel her way back. She was already so wet and disheveled it hardly seemed to matter that she tripped over a trailing plant and fell, and that low briers tangled her hair. She went without stopping until she was safely inside the garden door and had bolted it behind her. She put the lantern back by feel, and by feel she crept up the dark stairs and toward her own room.

At the top of the stairs as she looked up she saw, with a candle in its hand, a figure with a pale face framed in long dark hair, staring down at her. Nellie.

5

"You're awake," said Nellie, in a loud whisper. "You're not sleepwalking. I know, because you're looking at me properly."

"Of course I'm awake," said Florence. "Don't call Uncle Cris, or anything."

"Why should I call him—even if you were sleepwalking?" said Nellie. "Doctors can't cure sleepwalking. It's a nervous condition. Where've you been?"

"Out," said Florence. Her whisper was quieter than Nellie's.

"I can see that," said Nellie. "You're soaking. You must be making a wet patch on the stairs. Who did you go to see?"

"Nellie, shush," said Florence. "We can't talk here. People will hear us."

"They're asleep," said Nellie. "And if they weren't, they wouldn't hear us. Their doors are shut."

"That one isn't," said Florence. "Ferdy and Marcus. Their door's not shut."

"They always leave it open at night," said Nellie. "Ferdy's afraid of the dark, but Marcus won't let him have a night-light. Ferdy can see the outside lamp shine, from his bed. Their door doesn't mean anything."

"All the same," said Florence. "Come into my room."

To cut the argument short she led the way into her room and lit her candle; Nellie followed and shut the door behind them.

"Get that wet dressing gown off," said Nellie. "And your boots. Or you really will be ill."

"They'll never be dry by morning," said Florence, scrambling out of the wet things. "Even my nightgown's soaked. Move away from the chest of drawers while I find a dry one."

"People will say you've been sleepwalking again," said Nellie.

"I don't sleepwalk. I never did," said Florence.

"No. So who do you go to see?" said Nellie. "I know there's somebody. You aren't really interested in us; not like a real cousin. Not friends. There must be someone else. Is it a man?"

"Of course it's not a man," said Florence. "I want to be a proper cousin. Only I have things on my mind."

"Night visitors," said Nellie. "If it's not a man, is it a boy?"

"You'd give me away, if I told you," said Florence.

"No, I wouldn't," said Nellie. "Are you in love?"

"No," said Florence, slowly, feeling her way. "It isn't love. More like being under a spell. But actually, I don't want it. I'd rather have you—all of you," she added, as Nellie's stare narrowed into intensity. "And be young and have fun."

"Really?" said Nellie. "I'd rather be in love than anything. Where did you go?"

"I shan't tell you," said Florence.

"That means you're going again," said Nellie. "Suppose I did stop you. Suppose I told Father."

"You wouldn't," said Florence. "You said."

"I can watch, though," said Nellie. "Hear when you go out of your room, and go after you."

"Promise you won't," said Florence, desperately anxious. "As soon as I can—if I ever can—I'll tell you about it. So promise."

"I promise I won't follow you," said Nellie. "That's all."

To Florence, it sounded enough. She was cold, and tired, and still frightened. She said good-night to Nellie—suddenly stiff again, and "not like a cousin"; Nellie said good-night equally formally and went to her own bed. Florence rolled herself into a loop with her feet in her hands, to get warm under the patchwork quilt, and slept without dreaming.

The wet-skirted dressing gown and the still soggy boots were noticed by a maid doing a quick round of bed making before the family went to church; and Aunt Addy stopped Florence just as she was putting on her hat to go.

"Are you sure you want to come, Florence?" she asked. "Are you all right?"

"I'm perfectly all right," said Florence, hoping that shortage of sleep wasn't showing in a pale face or darkened eyes. "I'll come."

No more was said, but before lunch she heard Ferdy's whisper to Marcus behind a door. "Florence has been walking in her sleep again. Mother says we mustn't tell her we know; she said I mustn't tell you, too—but brothers forever."

"Brothers forever," repeated Marcus. "I won't say anything."

The number of curious stares Florence was subjected to at lunch warned her that most of the family knew something was up; they had, equally clearly, been warned not to talk to her about it. She wondered if Nellie had betrayed her. The promise had not included an outright statement that Nellie wouldn't talk to her father; and talking to her mother had never been mentioned.

Florence spent most of the day worrying about the night; and the casual kindness of Charles, and the fussy attentions of Isobel, were vaguely comforting. She had no conversation with Nellie, not even by looks—their eyes flicked apart as soon as they looked at each other.

The main event of the day was the discovery that Dolly had spent the night out, not in her stall, and was mysteriously lame. Mr. Tarrant, the groom, rubbed her legs and cosseted her, and Charles and Florence went to visit her with a gift of carrots, begged from Mrs. Rich.

"Dunno how she ever got out," said Mr. Tarrant. "She was put in her stall last night, and the half door bolted, see. None of the other horses got out. And how did she get into the paddock and shut the gate behind her? I ask you."

"I can't imagine, Mr. Tarrant," said Florence. But she feared she could, her mind's eye full of George and his knowing smile.

"Didn't Jacky hear anything?" asked Charles. Jacky, the stable-boy, slept—Florence realized—above the stables. Mr. Tarrant was a married man with a house in the village.

"He says not," said Mr. Tarrant. "I wonder if that chap's deaf, sometimes, I really do."

Florence wondered too, and rather hoped he was.

She saw that she had to be extra careful in her night visiting, and extra quick. It was more than likely that Aunt Addy, or Uncle Cris, would look in on her tonight.

To her relief, Aunt Addy visited, and visited early. Florence half waked to see Aunt Addy's face, looking soft and warm in her candle's light, and to feel Aunt Addy pull up the sheet and blanket and settle them over her shoulder.

"What is it?" Florence whispered.

"Nothing," said Aunt Addy. "I'm on my way to bed. Good-night, chick."

Florence vaguely wondered if Aunt Addy had called Nellie "chick" when she was a baby, and pictured the intense blue-eyed stare of the baby Nellie at such an endearment.

She didn't sleep again, but lay quietly until the whole house had been silent for some time—perhaps an hour. Then she put on her dressing gown (still damp and clinging—horrid) and slippers—she had decided that as boots got so rapidly soaked in the grass, she would leave her slippers at the door and go out barefoot.

As she felt her way along the corridor she was aware of a soft scuffling from Ferdy and Marcus's room; after she had gone a few more steps a board creaked behind her. She turned, afraid—quite illogically—that George was in the house. (How could he be? She'd never let him in.) But the two small shapes in the gleam of lamplight from outside were unmistakable.

"Marcus! Ferdy!" she whispered. "What are you doing?"

"Oh," said a disappointed voice. "You aren't asleep, are you? We wanted to see you sleepwalking."

"Don't be silly," said Florence coldly. "I'm going to the bathroom." She heard them creep disconsolately back to their room, and it was to the bathroom that she went.

She returned to her room and gave them half an hour to settle down; then tried again. This time, there was no disturbance, and she got herself down the stairs without a stumble, found the dark lantern where she had left it, padded softly to the little garden door, and slid back both the bolts. And turned the handle; and pulled. With no result. The door was locked.

A window, thought Florence. It would have to be a window. She tried the library first, and found the heavy sash window immovable. Uncle Crispin had at some time had locking devices fitted, and she remembered that Mr. Rich had a brass key for the window locks—and that all the windows on the ground floor had them. The upper floors hadn't, but the only creepers on the walls produced a map of small stalks and no good branches for climbing. Unless she broke a window, she was shut in the house.

Florence was not desperate enough to make great attempts to get out. She tried the garden door again, with the same results; so she slid its bolts home, put away the lantern, and returned to bed. She looked out of the bedroom window into the dark; but the room didn't face toward the paddock and meadow, only toward the wall of the stable yard. Nobody moved out there, as far as she could see; nothing and nobody.

"Sorry, George," she said to the blank dark. "I tried."

It was the second time, she thought, she had failed to say good-bye to George.

She slept well and heavily, though she did think once or twice, not quite waking, that she could hear a distant rattle and thump. She decided it was a thunderstorm and returned to dreamless peace.

Uncle Crispin and Mr. Rich both went down, from their different ends of the house, to see what the noise was, found nothing, and went dissatisfied to bed. There had been somebody or something outside, they were both sure.

6

For the next week, Aunt Addy kept Florence by her more than usual, and filled her time with talk and French lessons and visiting. Florence was glad of this, and said so.

"You're very kind, Aunt Addy," she said one day, as they drove back from a call on a neighbor. "I hope you don't get tired of having me around, but I like being with you. Company's nice."

"Yes, isn't it," said Aunt Addy, giving Florence a quick smile and looking back to Charlie-horse. "You'll have more of it soon. Only a week before Charles's holiday starts."

"Does he have longer holidays than the others, then?" asked Florence. "Isobel said they'd got three more weeks of school."

"Yes, he gets more; but he'll have holiday tasks to do," said Aunt Addy. "He won't do them, I'll wager. You'll find yourself much in demand. He's usually miserable as sin till the girls and the little boys are home."

"Will Isobel ever go to boarding school?" asked Florence.

"Not if your uncle can help it," said Aunt Addy. "He likes his Bel at home."

Florence thought sadly of her own father, still busy in Italy and saying nothing about his return. But Charles's company would be something of a compensation, she thought (and, more secretly—Charles would surely ward off by his mere presence any more visits from George?).

Dolly was having a long-drawn-out convalescence. Mr. Tarrant said she had strained a ligament; she was visited by a vet who recommended prolonged rest and keeping her in her stall.

"If she potters around in the field she'll only do it again," he said. "She's not so young as she was. Keep her boxed up a bit, Tarrant; it'll do no harm."

Florence got into the habit of visiting Dolly every day, with bits of apple or carrot or handfuls of sweet hay. She felt guilty about her—not that she felt that Dolly's injury was her fault, but because she had secret knowledge. She knew, and she wasn't saying, how Dolly had been hurt.

Once Charles was home, Florence guessed, her solitary visits to Dolly would stop. Charles, unlike the others, had a special liking for horses; he would come with Florence when she visited. She had grown fond of the quiet stable yard, with its cobbles onto which the box stalls opened, its carriage house, and its central well. She liked the clock mounted on a little turret above the hayloft, and the sundial in the wall beside the gate. On the last day before Charlie's holidays began, she lingered longer than usual to talk to Dolly.

"Sorry about you, Doll," she whispered to the old horse. "No, I haven't got anything else in my pockets.

Still lame, aren't you. Are you fed up with being in your stall all the time?"

"Not half as fed up as I am," said a hissing voice at the back of the stall. Florence jumped back, though Dolly didn't move. George was standing on the far side of Dolly's head.

"I wish you wouldn't keep sort of appearing," said Florence. "It's as if you wanted to frighten me."

"Perhaps I do," said George. "Why didn't you come? You're a liar and a cheat. You said you'd come out, and you never came."

"I did try, but I was locked in," said Florence. "All the doors and windows have locks on them, and the door I opened before was locked too. I couldn't get out."

"Oh, come on," said George. "You could have jumped. The upstairs windows aren't so high."

"Yes—and how should I have got back?" said Florence. "There aren't things to climb. I can't fly, George."

"A pity," said George. "I rattled at the doors, downstairs, and I threw earth at your window. You never answered. Didn't you hear?"

"Of course not," said Florence. "I was asleep. And if I had come to see you, George, it would have been to say good-bye. I'm not seeing you here."

"So you keep saying," said George. "I can't see why not. What harm will it do?"

"And I keep saying," said Florence, "people will see you. Any minute now, Mr. Tarrant and Jacky may come back from their tea. And the night when I didn't come, two of the boys were watching me."

"How do you know other people can see me?" said

George. He was taunting Florence, but she could not help answering him.

"Mr. Creed did," she said.

"He knew me before," said George. "Perhaps he was just remembering me."

"Other people knew you before," guessed Florence. "Didn't they? The aunts, of course; and Aunt Addy and maybe Uncle Cris. They might sort of remember, too. And now, Charles will be home all the time. He'll soon know if anything unusual is going on."

"Oh, Charles," said George contemptuously. "Why do you want Charles when you can have me?"

"Because he's real," shouted Florence, and stopped short, dismayed. That was something she had not meant to say; not meant even to think.

Instead of exploding at her, George dropped his voice to a whisper.

"And what am I, if I'm not real?" he said. "You've seen my photograph. You've got my knife. You've touched me. What do you think I am?"

"I don't think," said Florence. "You're George, and you're some sort of cousin, and I won't have you here, and that's the end of the whole story. Why won't you understand?"

"Oh, I understand," said George. "If you won't come out I'll rattle and bang the doors at night and throw things at the windows. And I'll make you come. You started it all and what's the point of backing out now— of being afraid? Come on—come now—we're going to the meadow. Jacky's rubbing Dinah down and Tarrant's not back from tea. We can slip by. Come on!"

He bounced on the balls of his feet, springing and eager. Florence followed him as far as the door of the stall; as far as the stable-yard gate; and then as he turned toward the meadow she turned toward the house and ran as fast as she could for the comfort and security of Mrs. Rich's sitting room.

That night, once again, there were disturbances outside the house, and a pane of glass in the garden door was broken with a stone. Charles got home from school next day, heard all about it, and was immensely excited.

"Somebody bears you a grudge," he said to his father. "It must be that. Burglars don't make a racket—they're all set to be as quiet as they can. There are Gypsies out on the common, Father. Could it be them?"

"They've no reason to bear me a grudge, Charles," said his father. "I haven't so much as spoken to them. They're perfectly harmless, anyway."

"Mrs. Blacket doesn't think so," said Audrey. "She thinks they took her gooseberries, before they were ever ripe, and she wanted them for gooseberry pie. And their dog chased Mr. Blacket's sheep." (Mrs. Blacket came in from the village once a week, to help with the laundry.)

"Spare us the village gossip, Audrey," said Aunt Addy.

"I don't care who it is, they mustn't get away with it," said Charles. "Let's sit up tonight, Father. We've got your rook-shooting gun, and my air gun. I expect Rich would sit up with us. If anyone comes around the house again, we'll shoot the blighter."

Florence was in torment. How could she say nothing, and wait for George to be shot down? If she spoke, what could she say? She was aware of Nellie's eyes on her, vividly watchful. She swallowed her feelings, and said nothing.

And that night, of necessity, she did nothing. She could think of no way to warn George.

Uncle Crispin had no intention of letting Charles sit up to shoot burglars, and packed him off to bed soon after the other children went; but he could not prevent Charles's jumping out of bed as soon as a noise was heard downstairs, hurrying down with his air gun and loosing off a pellet through the garden door—thus breaking another pane of glass. Uncle Crispin, Mr. Rich, and Charles then went around the outside of the house, with the dark lantern, to see whether anybody had been hit. They found nothing.

"Scared him off," said Charles triumphantly; but he still insisted on sitting on the top step of the stairs for the rest of the night, his air gun across his knees. He was found there, leaning asleep against the banisters, when Mrs. Rich came up with Aunt Addy's tea in the morning, and packed off to bed—where he slept right through breakfast, and nearly till lunch.

"We shan't hear anything of that chap again—you'll see," he said to Florence.

"I'm sure I hope not," said Florence.

It was quite true that there was no more banging around the house at nights. Charles felt proud of his guardianship, but Florence suffered from feelings that were hideously confused. Relief at the absence of disturbance and—apparently—the absence of George; guilt that George had been driven away by violence. And,

85

curiously, guilt that the happy life of Bellfield had once and for all shut George out. Inside were games and laughter and plentiful, perpetual bounties of food; outside was dark and damp and deprivation. Florence took to stealing occasional pieces of food—portable things like fruit or cake or buns—and leaving them secretly in the summerhouse. She settled her protesting conscience by eating less herself, and became known for refusing second helpings and asking for "only a little."

"Florence is off her food again," said Charles; and Nellie watched closely (even, Florence suspected, seeing the hiding-away of buns in pockets). Nobody else commented. The food disappeared from the summerhouse as soon as it was left there, and Florence grew very slightly thinner and paler.

For two weeks she reveled in Charles's almost undivided attention. He took her fishing, and although she refused to fish herself she discovered the joys of paddling in the shallow brook and dam building—one day the two of them built such a successful dam out of the brook's own stones that a flood rose and Mr. Blacket's cows were standing, bemused, in water (the children had to unmake that dam in a hurry before the farmer came for his cows at milking time). Charles took her bird's-nesting (to her relief, the nests were all empty by then); and she explored the small, dark wood the other side of the brook bridge, where yews and junipers grew among the lighter green of beech and lime trees. The two of them made a rope swing in the garden and Charles started on building a tree house, Florence's job being to pass planks up to him and pick up the hammer when he dropped it.

Charles was cheerful and undemanding, and she realized with surprise at the end of the second week that she had not felt frightened the entire time.

Also at the end of that week, when holidays for everyone began, it became clear that Florence was going with the Pearsons when they all went to Hastings for a seaside visit. She had the whole summer before she need think again of London and of George. She hoped it would never end.

7

When they were all back from Hastings, the salt washed out of their hair and the sand shaken out of their clothes and the sunburn faded down to a pale toast color, the expected letter came from Aunt Dorrit and Aunt James (signed by them both; but Aunt James, who was the businesswoman of the two, had written it). Florence's school started on September thirteenth; and when was she to be expected back in London, and should the aunts meet her? And would Adela (Aunt Addy) please send Florence's waist measurement and height, in case her school skirts needed altering before term began?

Florence sighed, and drooped a little over the breakfast table, when this letter was commented on and the aunts' kind messages passed on to her.

"They so much look forward to having you home, and send love and kisses," said Isobel, reading over her mother's elbow.

"Don't you want to go?" asked Nellie. "Your own school, and your friends again?"

"My friends aren't terribly special friends," said Florence. "School's all right, but I can't pretend I miss it."

"Florence likes us best," said Audrey smugly.

"I suppose the aunts don't say when my father's coming home?" asked Florence.

"I'm afraid they don't mention it," answered Aunt Addy. "But surely it must be soon?"

"You never know, with him," said Florence.

Florence started mentally crossing off the days before her return to London, looking every day at the colorful calendar in Nellie and Audrey's room. Nellie caught her doing this one day.

"Don't you really want to go?" she asked.

"No, I don't," said Florence. "It would be different if Daddy were home. It isn't that I'm not fond of the aunts. . . . "

"But there are things you're afraid of," said Nellie.

"How do you know?" asked Florence.

"You show it," said Nellie. "Why don't you tell somebody? Somebody could stop it."

"I don't know if they could," said Florence.

"Well then, stop it yourself," said Nellie. "Father's planning to take you on the tenth. You haven't got long."

"You'll have your own room back," said Florence.

"That doesn't matter," said Nellie, and Florence was surprised to see that she meant it.

As September began, so bad dreams began for Florence. She had never had dreams like these before. They were mostly dreams about the Paragon. The house was always in darkness; and she was always hiding or running from something or somebody. Sometimes the house in the dream had extra floors, or other features that the Paragon didn't have—cellars, balconies, towers, spiral staircases. Always the dreams were horrible, and one or two of them were ridiculous. In one the bottom of the house was full of water, but when she looked into it there was no reflection and she could not see her own face. She had to jump into it to escape from Mr. Creed, who was behind her shouting words she could not hear.

On the ninth of September, a still, silent day of tranquil brightness, Florence was alone again. The girls and the younger boys had already started school; Uncle Crispin had gone for a day's rook shooting and taken Charles to help fetch and carry, and perhaps get a shot or two. Mrs. Rich was doing a grand ironing and mending for Florence, and Aunt Addy had started sorting out the things that were to be packed for her. Florence wandered the garden, hardly seeing the sheaves of Michaelmas daisies and the firework-like chrysanthemums, the fat and busy spiders in their geometrical webs. Her panic left her dry-throated and headachy. She had in her pinafore pocket the photograph of George, and his knife—which whoever did her packing must not see.

Dolly was out in the paddock again now, allowed to wander as she pleased; but Florence still liked and visited the stable yard. Her steps took her there at midday, when it was deserted—Mr. Tarrant and Jacky were at their dinner and the rook shooters had taken Dinah and Charlie-horse to drive and ride. The cover was off the well (a heavy round of wooden slats, which Florence couldn't have lifted), and buckets and brooms standing by suggested that the men had gone off to eat in the middle of washing down the yard. Florence hung over the rim of the well and stared at her face in the dark water. The stable clock began to strike twelve and on a sudden impulse, she took the knife from her pocket and dropped it into the depths. "Go away—go—go—go," she said rapidly, twelve times, as the clock struck; and as it finished striking she turned and went off to the paddock and to Dolly without looking back.

Uncle Crispin and Charles came back in the late afternoon; Florence heard the horses and went around to the stable yard to meet them. They were pleased with themselves and jolly, boasting about how well they had shot.

"The Squire said to me, 'Not so bad for a beginner,'" Charles said to Florence. "Father was marvelous, though; he shot dozens. Rook pie tomorrow!"

"Not so much talk, my lad," said Uncle Crispin. "See to the horses first. Tarrant! Jacky! The trough's empty and these nags need watering. Get a bucket to the well."

"Yes, sir, right away," called out Jacky. "We've got the top off ready."

His feet clattered cheerfully on the cobbles, and his busy voice muttered to the bucket, "Down you go then—that's the way"—and changed suddenly into a wordless shout as he looked over the well's edge into the depths.

"What's amiss?" called Tarrant, and Uncle Crispin bellowed, "Get on with it, man!"

Jacky found his voice. "It's a body, sir," he wailed. "Oh Doctor—Doctor—sir—there's a body in the well!"

Tarrant and Uncle Crispin and Charles raced to the well, elbowing Jacky out of their way, and craned over the edge.

"It's a child," said Uncle Crispin. "A boy, I think," and Tarrant burst out, "He's a goner, for sure, Doctor. Drowned like a kitten."

Her last meal seemed to rise up in Florence's throat, but she swallowed hard and managed not to vomit. She wanted, and did not want, to run to the well; but her hands and feet seemed impossible to move.

"We've got to try, men," said Uncle Crispin. "Get him up quick. Get ropes, Tarrant. Charles, get a couple of hooks from the tack room. Florence—run to the house, will you; tell Mrs. Rich to get blankets out and put water to heat. Run, Florence, run!"

His sharp order seemed to unfreeze Florence from her immobility and she set off running to the house. The stable-men, and Charles, had already rushed into the buildings, and the horses stood forgotten by the empty trough.

Mrs. Rich would have kept Florence in the house, seeing her pale and sweaty with shock and speed. But Florence insisted she must go back to the stable yard— "There may be more messages for me to carry," she said. She got as far as the garden door of the house and stopped then, seeing Uncle Crispin coming; so she was watching when he carried the body in. It was undoubtedly a boy. Water dripped from the legs and the black boots dangling over the doctor's left arm, and against his right arm sagged a white face, black hair plastered to it. He carried the dead George into the house, into his surgery; and although Florence knew he would fight with artificial respiration for as long as he thought right she also knew that it would be no use. The body he carried was a drowned body; its photograph was in her pocket and its knife at the bottom of the well. She was shocked, but not surprised, when her uncle came later into the dining room where all the family were together, pretending to eat tea, and said to her aunt, "No use, my dear. I did my best, but the boy's gone. There never was any real hope. He could have been in that well since midday; the men admit they left the cover off it all afternoon."

"What a tragic thing," said Aunt Addy, her eyes wet. "My dear, who is he? Is it one of the village boys?"

"A stranger to me. Respectably dressed, but I do just wonder if he's a Gypsy child," said Uncle Crispin. "They're back on the common, aren't they? And he's very dark."

"Shall I look myself?" Aunt Addy asked.

"Later," said Uncle Crispin. "We'll have our tea. He's in my surgery. And I've sent Jacky to inform the constable."

As soon as she had drunk a cup of tea and eaten a slice of bread and butter, Aunt Addy went quietly off to see whether she recognized the dead boy. She came back a few minutes later, in a great hurry.

"Crispin, he's gone. The body's gone," she said.

"What!" said Uncle Crispin. "How can it be? He was stone dead, Addy."

"I'm not disputing that," said Addy. "The wet blankets

are there, where you put him. Somebody must have come and taken him away."

"Gypsies, then; it must be. Who else would just take away a corpse without a word? And what the blazes do I tell Constable Mather?" said Uncle Crispin. "I'd better go and look."

"Yes, you'd better," said Aunt Addy; and Nellie asked, casually, "Was he real?"

"Oh yes, he was real, Nell," said Uncle Crispin. "Solid flesh and blood, not a changeling. I carried him."

"You'd better look at Florence, when you get back," said Nellie. "I think she's fainted."

"She was there when we found him; she saw most of it," said Charles. "No wonder she's upset."

Florence had no recollection of being taken up to her room and put to bed; and she had to be told much later about the fuss in the village about the missing body, and Constable Mather's annoyance.

"He did ought to have been watched," said Constable Mather. "We can't have an inquest without the corpse— now can we, Doctor? Coroner wouldn't allow it. Corpses shouldn't be let wander off all anyhow."

"He was dead, and if I'd had his name I'd have written his death certificate," said Uncle Crispin shortly. "That means he was taken, and that means the Gypsies. You'd better talk to them. And if I'm completely wrong and he wasn't dead at all—well, you've a case to investigate."

"There's a case all right," said Constable Mather. "If the body's just gone and no word said, then you can be sure somebody wanted him dead. It's a suspicious circumstance."

Somebody wanted him dead. Nellie, sitting unnoticed and listening in a corner, heard and went away wondering. Aunt Addy had put Florence to bed and was staying with her; Nellie, unusually helpful, offered to take down to Mrs. Rich any of Florence's clothes that were for the wash. Halfway down the stairs she slid the photograph out of the pinafore pocket, looked at it speculatively, and pocketed it herself. A little later she was back in Florence's room.

"Are you going to telegraph to the aunts, Mother?" she asked. "You can't send Florence back tomorrow, can you?"

"No, I'm sure I can't," said Aunt Addy. "She still hasn't properly waked, and it's a bit worrying. Can you get your cycle and ride down to the post office? There'll still be somebody about."

"What shall I put?" said Nellie.

"'Illness Florence delayed,'" said Aunt Addy. "Can you find my address book, for the address? And have you got enough money?"

"Don't worry, I can manage. You just think about Florence," Nellie said. "Ma—Florence won't die too, will she?"

"Of course not, Nellie. She's almost awake—her eyelids flickered then," said Aunt Addy.

In her brief moment of near-consciousness Florence had heard the words "Florence won't die too, will she?" and had heard the urgent tone behind them. Something comforting reached her, even through the fogging in her mind. Perhaps she was dying, as George had died. But Nellie—Nellie would be sorry if she did.

8

Florence's illness was long and violent. There were patches when she was awake and understood what was happening, when Uncle Crispin would reassure her that it was "just a fever—a nasty go—but she was no end better," or when a trained nurse who was imported into the house to look after her would wash her and feed her beef tea or calves'-foot jelly with a teaspoon. Between these intervals she dreamed: not nightmares now, but long, drifting dreams where she was in a garden with George, by the brook with Charles, making daisy chains with Audrey, doing her homework in the Paragon with the aunts sitting by. George was there often: not a threatening George, but a playful and sometimes plaintive George, accompanied by a scent of lilacs. In one of the waking moments Isobel leaned over the bed and whispered, "Flo—your father's coming. He'll be here on Thursday. There!"—as Florence weakly smiled—"I knew you'd be pleased."

Florence hardly knew whether she was pleased or not. "I'm critically ill—my father's been sent for," said one anxious level of her thoughts. Another level just said "Daddy" and knew that to see him was what she wanted.

All the troubles could be told, the difficulties smoothed away; he was the answer to it all.

She related her father's being sent for to words of Uncle Crispin's, spoken to Aunt Addy and the nurse when they thought she was asleep: "There'll be a crisis; soon, I expect. It may go either way. She mustn't be left alone and if there seems to be any change, I must be called. At once."

"Yes, Doctor," said the nurse's tidy voice, and Florence's dreams took over once again.

That evening—she believed it was the evening of the same day—she woke suddenly, free of dreams and confusion, her mind a busy spin of meanings and purposes. George was drowned, and in some way it was her fault. Certainly she hadn't pushed him into the well; but she had willed him to go and had never translated what "go" meant. And the Gypsies, it seemed, had taken him. (Why? For his good clothes? Stories were told of their stealing children and taking their clothes for their own families, sending the stolen children home in rags; but would they touch the dead?)

There was only one way to make sure what had happened, that George was really gone; and that was to go to the Gypsy encampment and to ask. If George was there, she would know him even in flea-infested rags, and know the truth. And know she must.

The nurse was dozing in her chair, set in the window where the late sunlight touched it. Florence judged it must be about six o'clock. The pool of brightness made the room extremely hot, and Florence did not think of putting on either boots or dressing gown. Even her night-dress—a starched white cotton, with frills and pin tucks—seemed almost too great a weight of clothing. She went out without waking the nurse, down and through the silent house. The children must all be together some-where, playing or doing their prep. for tomorrow; Aunt Addy and Uncle Cris perhaps having a short time of peace in the drawing room. The servants would all be about their evening work: making a start on the prepara-tions for dinner, disposing of the remains of tea.

Florence went out of the front door, picked her way across the gravel of the drive, and went barefoot onto the grass and its drifted leaves (Why so many? How long had she been ill? The branches arching the driveway now were almost bare).

The common was a tract of land between the village and the meadows that fringed the brook and the hillside with its hanging wood; it was heathy and scrubby and a won-derful place for rabbits and birds. Florence walked there so fast that she hardly noticed what was under her bare feet: the tangled meadow grass, the gravel and stones of the track, the twiggy sharpness of heather. By the time she reached the common, the evening chill had set in and a small mist was rising from the river; she was not aware either of the passing of time or the sensation of cold.

The common seemed to be empty: there were no Gypsy vans, no hobbled horses, no groups of people talk-ing and smoking around fires, no dogs. But yes—one dog, bounding toward her, and one man, dark-haired and brown-skinned, following the dog, a bag slung over his shoulder. He stopped and stared at Florence.

"Where are the Gypsies?" asked Florence. "Isn't this their camp?"

"All gone, Miss," said the man. "Up and off this afternoon. I'm the last of them, and I'm off now too. I only stayed because my dog went lost."

Florence noted the bulging of the bag on his back, and thought it more likely he'd stayed for a spot of rabbiting.

"There was a boy—drowned," she said.

"Ah. Not one of us. Police came asking—they would. Folk blame us for everything—first thing they think of. He wasn't one of ours, though. And so we told 'em."

"You didn't—take him away?" asked Florence.

"What for?" said the man. "What'd be the use? You his sister, then?"

"No," said Florence.

"Ah," said the man. "I heard he was a stranger; nobody knew him. You, now, I know who you are. Up at the doctor's, and if I don't offend, you ought to get back there right off. Out in your nightclothes—'tisn't fit."

"I'm going," said Florence, and abruptly turned her back on him. He stood between her and the path that led to Bellfield, and in her embarrassment she walked not toward home but toward the brook and the wood. He shouted after her, but she didn't turn her head.

The bridge over the brook was a plank one, with a handrail at one side. To give the Gypsy time to go away, and herself time to know what she should do next, she loitered on this bridge looking down into the water, darkening as the daylight started to fade. Below her was a pool where the brook moved more sluggishly, and her face was reflected there—a pale blur above the brighter pallor of her frilled collar. As she looked, another face appeared beside her own, broken and a little distorted by the ripples of the midstream flow. For a moment she thought of the Gypsy; but as the water slackened for a moment and the ripples stilled, she knew it was George.

9

"This time," said George's voice behind her, "you came to me! Always I've had to come to you. This time you came looking." The voice seemed—for a moment—to come from the mouth of the mirrored face, to be a voice underwater.

"I had to know if you were drowned," said Florence. "They said you were. Uncle Crispin said so."

"But you knew I couldn't be," said George. His voice now sounded normal, lively and teasing.

"I half thought you were. And I half knew you couldn't be," said Florence. She turned and looked at him. Same old George—bright, mocking, menacing. The same fascination, the same fear. No signs of water.

"So this time," said George, "we'll do what I want to."

"I thought we always did," said Florence. "You always choose."

"Maybe; but I choose what you want," said George. (Florence felt that this was monstrously untrue.) "Come on now, time we went."

"Where are we going?" asked Florence, hanging back.

"To the wood. To the trees," said George.

"But it will be all rough and prickly there, and I've got nothing on my feet," said Florence.

"No—ferns and moss, and fallen leaves," said George.

"And cold," insisted Florence.

"You won't feel cold," said George. He took her hand and pulled her after him, across the bridge, through the soft meadow, toward the dark hanging wood and its heavy trees. Florence resisted at first, but she was aware of the strength of his pull, of the energy that emanated from him. He seemed to have lost the sadness, the reluctance, she had sometimes sensed in him; he seemed all drive and motion.

They went into the wood not by a path but where a trickle of water from a spring ran down over slippery stones; it was, as George had said, mossy and ferny. The intense cold, gripping now as night came down, had frozen the running water into stillness and fingers of ice, and made the woodland leaf mold firm underfoot. Florence was not aware of the cold in her own limbs. She felt only a stiffness and a numbness. She must, she thought, be past the teeth-chattering stage.

It seemed to her to be hours that they wandered in the wood. George told her to be quiet when she asked questions, and he heaved her up icy, sliding places and towed her through fern and bramble patches at a steady, irresistible pace. He was sure of his path; that at least was a relief to her.

He did stop once, when Florence tripped over a loop of root, and fell; he pulled her up and waited for her to get her breath, leaning, himself, against the trunk of a tall beech tree.

Florence shook dead leaves from her skirt and brushed them out of her hair.

"Why is it so cold, George, and so dark, and why are the leaves all down?" she asked.

"It's late," said George.

"Isn't it September?" asked Florence.

"Deep winter and deep night," said George. "You were ill for weeks. There will be hard frost tonight. It's freezing now. Only you don't feel it."

"I can't feel anything anymore," said Florence. "Aren't we almost there?"

"We are there," said George. "Look."

He turned her by the shoulders, and she saw—through branches and by what light the stars gave—ruined walls, fallen masonry, a window square empty of glass, a gaping doorway; around them the dark patching of nettles and elder scrub.

"A house," said George. "Shelter. You can get warm. You'll like that."

"But it's a ruin," said Florence, stumbling toward it. "It hasn't been a house for years."

"Oh no, it's a house," said George. "There are still flowers around it—primroses and periwinkle. And roses gone back to the brier. Feel with your feet—here's the doorstep. Come inside."

"I couldn't," exclaimed Florence, standing on the step and hanging on by the doorposts as George tried to tug her in. "It's dark as the pit, and sort of dead. It feels like a tomb. And it smells."

"It just smells like a house," said George.

"It doesn't," said Florence. "It smells of rot and mold. I'm not going in."

"We'll have a light," said George. There was niche in

the stone halfway up the wall to the right of the door, as if one stone had fallen out. He pulled out from there matches and a candle stub, lit the candle, and stood it in the niche. His hand went into his pocket and came out holding the silver knife.

"Look," he said to Florence. "This is what it's always been for. I cut your hand—just a small cut—then I cut mine and we hold hands. Our blood mingles. Then we're blood brother and sister; we're the same tribe, forever and ever."

"What for?" said Florence.

"When we've done it, we shall be the same: You'll see what I see," said George. "Not a ruined house at all, but a strong one standing up with all its doors and windows, with a fire burning and a kettle singing, furniture in it—chairs and cushions, cups and saucers—food in the cupboard and a bird in a cage."

"I don't believe you," said Florence.

"You'll see it with your own eyes," said George, reaching for her hand.

"No," said Florence. She turned her hands into clenched fists and held them down at her sides.

"I'll cut your wrist, then," said George, reaching for her arm. "It doesn't matter where."

The faint gleam of the candlelight caught his eyes and Florence was afraid of the shine in them. Panic overwhelmed her and rose choking to her throat, and nerved her with a sudden ferocity. She jumped at George, prized open his fingers to grab the knife, jabbed it toward his chest, and turned and ran. She heard George cry out and knew she had hit him somewhere; but she was too afraid of him now to stay and investigate. She stumbled and slithered and crashed her way through the wood, crying in exhaustion and in fear, until she fell at last out of the last of the ferns and the brambles and stood, shaken by shuddering, in the river meadow with her feet on level ground.

She had only one thought in her head, now, and that was to get home: to run and run until the lights of Bellfield showed through the night and the frost, and she could find people and ordinariness and the reassurance of talk. The village was quiet as she ran through it, but the houses had lamps and candles lit inside. Not a dog barked at her, and nobody was about in the streets. She was reasonably sure that she got back to Bellfield unobserved; the villagers wouldn't all be talking, next day, about how the doctor's niece ran around in her night things, and barefoot, no better than she ought to be.

Florence halted when she got to the front door of the house. If she knocked or rang there, so late, Uncle Crispin might come, expecting that the caller had come to fetch him to a patient. He was not the person she wanted to see first. She would rather meet Mrs. Rich first—and get a drink of hot milk, a clean nightdress, and her feet washed before she faced the family. She went on, limping and slow now that she could think about being home, around to the back. There was a light showing under the solid back door that led to the servants' quarters, and she could hear the hum of talk from inside. Mr. and Mrs. Rich were there, and Jacky, and at least one of the maids. Full of hope and relief, Florence hammered on the door.

As she had expected, it was Mrs. Rich who came. The door was flung wide open and the rosy light of the kitchen fire and the bright lamp flooded out to where Florence stood.

Mrs. Rich screeched, a long incoherent scream bubbling at last into words. "It's her—it's her ghost—it's her ghost! She's away!" she babbled wildly. The door banged to with a crash, and Florence heard the bolts rammed home.

10

A ghost. Her own ghost. Florence turned away from the house, shaking. Bellfield had rejected her; she for her part had rejected George. She belonged nowhere: not in his world, nor in the world she still called real. She was nothing and nobody and she had nowhere at all to go.

She wandered first in the garden and grounds of Bellfield, hoping to find some token somewhere that she still had a part in this place. The house cat ran past and didn't stop to be fondled, but jumped up on the wall of the stable yard and was gone. The horses in their stalls barely turned to look at her, though she did feel a little comforted by the warmth of their breath.

She walked to the village again, slowly now, and went—as if inevitably drawn—to the churchyard. A ghost—how long a ghost? She searched the headstones, reading as the moonlight grew stronger the names chiseled into them. Was there one somewhere that said FLORENCE WHEATCROFT and some date or other when she died? The blades of grass she trod on were rimmed with frost, and crunched; the ivy on the stones had frost frills around its leaves. Her name was not there, but that was small consolation. Perhaps she was buried in London—would her father have taken her there?

It seemed to her hours that she hunted in the church-yard, hours that she wandered around the village looking at the white gardens and the darkened windows—shuttered, curtained, or staring blank now that the occupants were all in bed and the lamps all out. At last she realized that a grayness was coming into the air and the moonlight fading; dawn was beginning.

A new day; and if she had only just died, perhaps her father would come, and find her not there. The other children would talk to him, Nellie would stare at him. Perhaps he would take Nellie on the arm of his chair, call her by pet names, because—the only dark one—she would be the most like his own lost daughter?

Florence's self-pitying imaginings were swept away in anger and jealousy. If her father was coming, she herself would be there, even if she could be no more than a haunting presence. She would get into Bellfield somehow.

Bellfield, when she got back to it, showed a few lights. The one over the door—a gas lamp—burned pale in the growing light, and there was a faint twinkle from Nellie and Audrey's room and from her own bedroom. She avoided the front door as before, and this time the back door too. She went straight to the garden door, with some thought in her head that she might use George's knife—still in her hand—to pick the lock. She had forgotten the bolts. But when, acting by guess alone, she turned the handle and pushed on the door, it simply gave and she walked through. It was almost as though it was not a solid door at all; but it sounded real enough as it shut behind her.

With the windows all shimmering and gray, she didn't need a light in the passages or on the stairs. She went to her own room; the door stood ajar and there by the window was Aunt Addy, standing looking out at the faint shapes of the garden. She was fully dressed and her shoulders sagged as if she were tired. Not to attract her attention, Florence slid soft-footed toward the bed.

There was somebody in the bed. Startled but not afraid, Florence saw her own sleeping face and the tangle of her hair on the pillow.

There was only one thing to be done. Florence slipped the knife under the pillow, climbed into bed beside the sleeper, who was firm and warm, and lost herself in depth and dreamlessness.

11

Florence woke in full daylight, with morning sun glittering on the windowpane; and she woke to a full recollection of all that had happened. The fears of the night broke over her like a wave and washed away. She was Florence; she was alone in the bed; she was warm and comfortable, except where her feet and ankles ached and stung.

There was no nurse in the room, and no Aunt Addy. But there was a noise of crying—passionate, tearing sobs. Nellie, in her dressing gown, was lying face down across the foot of the bed, her head buried in her arms; and the crying was hers.

"Nellie!" said Florence. Her voice seemed strange to her, shaking and husky. She tried again. "Nellie! What's wrong?"

Nellie sprang to her feet, staring at Florence; then leaped to her and touched her cheek, seized her hands and kissed them.

"You're alive!" she exclaimed. "You're alive! Oh, Florence, I thought you were dead. It was all my fault, and you were dead."

"I think I thought so, too," said Florence. "Why did you?"

"Late last night, Mrs. Rich said she'd seen your fetch," said Nellie. "She had hysterics, on and on for hours."

"What's a fetch?" said Florence, afraid that she knew.

"It's like your ghost," said Nellie. "It appears when you're dying. People used to say it had come to fetch you. She saw it outside, all in white. It came to the door for you."

"What did everybody else think?" asked Florence.

"She scared us stiff," said Nellie. "Me and Isobel and the boys, at least. Father thought you really might die, last night; he said it would go one way or the other. He and Mummy both sat up, to help the nurse, and we were all sent to bed. But I couldn't sleep. I looked out of the window, in the middle of the night, and I saw you—out on the lawn, looking up at the house. So I went down and unlocked the garden door and pulled the bolts back. Mrs. Rich thought the one outside was a ghost and the one inside was you. But I'd looked in at your door when I went to bed, and you were so still and so white I thought perhaps the one inside was the ghost and the one outside might be you. I came just now to see how you were, and I couldn't see you breathing and there was nobody else here and I thought they'd gone and left you because it was no use anymore, and I'd let in the wrong one and you'd died because of it."

"Untuck the bed at the bottom, Nellie," said Florence. "Look at my feet."

Florence's feet, when they showed between the sheets, were streaked with dirt and gray-blue with bruises; scratches jagged them here and there.

"I was the one outside, Nellie," whispered Florence. "You let me in."

The two smiled at each other, long satisfying smiles.

"You'd better wash your feet yourself," said Nellie. "I'll smuggle you in some hot water when nobody's around.

I'm sure I can get off school today; I'll say I didn't sleep."

"Tell me about the key," said Florence. "Was it you who locked the door up earlier? Why?"

"I've had the key a long time," said Nellie. "I took it last summer, when the nights were hot; I liked to go outside when everyone thought I was in bed. They thought the key was lost, and they had to leave the door unlocked and use the bolts. Father kept meaning to get another key, and kept forgetting. I kept it hidden. When I found you were going outside at night, and wouldn't tell me why, I thought I'd stop you."

"You did," muttered Florence.

"Miss Florence! You're awake!" said the nurse's pleased voice as she came in carrying a jug of hot water. "You're so much better today, and I've come to give you a nice hot wash. That's enough talk for now, Miss Nellie. You can come back later—if the doctor says you're allowed."

"Yes, nurse," said Nellie. She gave Florence a wink that filled her with a tingle of delight, and went off skipping.

"I won't talk if you don't want me to," said Florence to the nurse. "But do just tell me—has my father come?"

"He should be here this evening," said the nurse. "So save your talking for him."

"And what day is it?" asked Florence.

"November the first," said the nurse. "Halloween last night, and it's my belief somebody in this house was pulling somebody else's leg—but there, it wasn't you, poor lamb, ill as you were."

"Don't you believe in ghosts?" said Florence. "I do."

"Of course I don't, dear. Stuff and nonsense," said the nurse.

Florence gave up and let herself be washed. The nurse never thought of looking at her feet, which stayed as they were until Nellie kept her promise and smuggled some more hot water in.

Florence's recovery was slow, and happened in odd jerks. For the first few days she hardly had the energy for much talk, and became breathless if she talked too long or if anybody made her laugh. She learned she had had pneumonia; her father told her that, when he first came up, the moment he arrived at Bellfield, to kiss and cuddle her. She certainly hadn't the breath then to start him on a long conversation about George.

But on a later occasion she turned the talk that way. She was allowed out of bed by then, but not out of the bedroom, and she was sitting in an armchair that her uncle had carried in, well propped by cushions.

"You've been ill such weeks, my poor girl," her father said, "first with some sort of fever your uncle didn't understand, then this pneumonia. I was frightened stiff when I heard about it, and came galloping home like a stampeding elephant."

"I've been frightened, too," began Florence.

"I'm sure you were," said her father. "I'm told you were delirious—your mind was wandering."

"But what frightened me, Daddy, was George," said Florence with determination. "Georges Valery. I want you to tell me about him, please."

"How the blazes did you come across him?" asked her

father. "Do people dig that story up, still? I thought he was forgotten."

"Nobody dug him up," said Florence. "I found his photograph, and then his knife—in the table drawer in the Paragon."

"And he haunts your dreams?" said her father. "Well, he was a fetching fellow. More attractive to girls than was good for him. Or them."

"Daddy, I kept seeing him," said Florence. "And that last night, when I was very ill, I went after him."

"You were delirious, Flo," said her father. "Rambling. He wasn't really there."

"He was, Daddy," said Florence. "And lots of times before. I saw him at the Paragon."

"You had strange dreams at the Paragon," said her father. "And walked in your sleep. The aunts mentioned it in their letters, and I wondered if I should come home. But I stopped worrying when I heard you'd come to Bellfield. You weren't seeing a real Georges, child. Georges is dead."

"Not the one I saw," said Florence.

"It's called a hallucination," said her father gently. "It seems absolutely real, but only one person can see it."

"Mr. Creed saw George," said Florence. "He said there'd been a boy in the garden."

"The world's full of boys," said her father. "Some lad got over the wall, probably. For a dare; or looking for apples to scrump."

Not in the spring, thought Florence. She tried again.

"Do believe me, Daddy," she said. "It's the truth. He kept coming to the Paragon and I thought he wouldn't follow me here—but he did. It was because of him I fell off Dolly, and Dolly went lame; and I leave him food in the garden, and he takes it. And, Daddy, it was his body in the well."

"Look, my dear," said her father, still patient but now very firm. "A lot of things have happened to upset you. The sleepwalking business, and your accident, and seeing a dead body—a dreadful thing to happen to a little girl—and pneumonia on top of it. It's no wonder your mind is in a tangle."

"I'm not a little girl," said Florence feebly. "My mind's not tangled."

"I'm not saying I don't believe you," said her father. "I believe every word you say. But our own thoughts can deceive us; young people especially are prone to dreams and fancies. It's likely to happen to somebody like you, who has had a lot to suffer very young. I don't forget that, Florence. All those months—I could almost say years—when your mother was so ill and we both tried to keep cheerful and help each other along: It was a lot to ask of you, and perhaps you're paying the price for it now. So try to be strong, as you were strong then—to help me—and put these ideas behind you. You're still a child; just enjoy that, and have fun, and don't let your imagination run away with you and spoil your happiness."

Florence was close to tears now. She could only nod and let the conversation end. It was hard to remember her mother's long illness; it was hard to be made to feel her present troubles were not only made by herself, but were even a kind of selfishness. She knew she would not tackle her father again about George. His mere presence was a comfort; but he was not going to give her the necessary comfort of believing her.

Somebody did believe her, though, and it was Nellie.

The joy of Florence's recovery—besides her father's company—was Nellie. Nellie came to see her every day, and talked, telling Florence what was going on in the house, what Audrey had said that had made the family laugh, what she had done at school. Nellie, the silent, chattered like a sparrow. Florence wondered at first if Nellie was making an effort, to relieve an invalid; but she came to realize that Nellie actually wanted to talk. More, Nellie told her amusing stories, Nellie imitated her teachers, Nellie was heard to giggle. When Florence's nurse was dismissed, Nellie suggested moving her own bed into Florence's room. To her mother she said, "Florence might need something in the night. She might walk in her sleep. I'd wake up; I'd see she was all right."

Aunt Addy came up alone to see Florence, when Florence had gone early to bed, to consult her about this.

"How do you feel about Nellie's sleeping in here?" she asked. "Tell me truly, Florence. Is it what you want? I know it's what Nellie wants. But you?"

"Yes, I do, Aunt Addy," said Florence. "I'd feel sort of safer. And it's funny—I thought Nellie didn't like me much, but now we're like best friends."

"Yes, I know," said Aunt Addy. "It's the best thing that's ever happened to Nellie. She's always wanted a best friend. Sometimes a friendship started, but then the other child moved away; Nellie's had several heartbreaks. She's the passionate one; her heart breaks much too easily. It's made her cautious. And of course she's been lonely."

"I can't imagine being lonely here," said Florence. "Such a big family, so much going on."

"Nellie and Isobel haven't a lot in common, and have never been real friends," said Aunt Addy. "Isobel's such a busy little person, and she's got no time for dreams and stories and imaginings. Audrey's like her. They're the practical ones. Isobel and Charles have always been hand in glove, too, and Nellie's felt left out. She's got quieter and quieter, and it's not good. You make her talk, Florence; you'll do so much good."

"I can't stop her talking," said Florence. Nellie's bed was moved that evening, and Aunt Addy had to come in to tell the two girls to be quiet, and get some sleep, at half past ten.

Not that night, but a few nights later, they were lying half asleep after an hour or so of conversation. They had been reciting together their favorite verses out of *English Ballads,* especially parts of "The Demon Lover" and "The Outlandish Knight," which they both thought the most terrifying poems in the book. Florence had got over her cold shivers and come out from under the blankets, where she had buried her head, when she was startled fully awake by the sound of footsteps going around the house. She sat up, listening, and heard Nellie move in her bed.

"Listen!" said Florence. "There's somebody out there."

"It'll be Mr. Rich," said Nellie. "He goes around outside every night, since we had those disturbances."

"Oh," said Florence, immensely relieved. "I thought it might be George." She realized at once that she had been indiscreet.

"So that's his name," said Nellie. "George what?"

"Georges Valery," said Florence.

"Who is he?" Nellie demanded.

"I knew him in London," said Florence. "But Daddy says it's a hallucination. He says he's dead."

"Who was he, then?" said Nellie.

"Some sort of relation," said Florence. "He said the great-aunts, in London, were his aunts. They had his photograph. My father had his knife."

"The one that was under your pillow," said Nellie.

"So it was," said Florence. "I don't know where it is now."

"It fell on the floor," said Nellie. "I hid it for you; it's in your drawer, where it was before. I ought to tell you, Florence—I looked in that drawer. I knew you had a secret. Is it George in the photograph that was there?"

"Yes," said Florence. "I don't know where that is now, either."

"I put that back, too," said Nellie. "It was in your pinafore pocket. How did George come?"

"I made him come," said Florence. "I called him. At first it was fun. Now it's all too difficult. I think I don't want to talk about him. It makes me remember too much. It makes it real."

"All right," said Nellie. But she went next day to the attic and hunted through some of the boxes up there until she found the old family photograph albums. She leafed through these until she found a particular photograph. She couldn't loosen it from its mount so she took the whole page—a small one—downstairs with her and hid it inside *English Ballads.* She was keeping it for reference.

12

Nothing more was said for a while about Florence and her father's return to London, and Florence's return to school. But as Florence grew stronger she realized that these things could not be put off forever. When her father called her to walk in the garden, one still December day, she felt sure she knew what he was going to say.

"Nearly the end of term, Flo," he said as they walked side by side along the path and looked at a few late roses, fragile but bright. "You've missed nearly two terms of school."

"Yes, I know," said Florence. "I'm quite scared of going back. The others will be miles ahead of me."

"You needn't be scared," said her father. "You'll catch up all right. Are there other reasons why you don't want to go back?"

Florence was shocked into silence. Had Nellie reopened the subject of George; and had Nellie been believed? "What do you mean?" she whispered.

"Well, it's an odd life for a child—just you and the aunts," said her father. "A bit lonely for you, isn't it? Haven't you liked the company here—Aunt Addy, and the young ones giving life a bit of fun?"

"Yes, I have liked it," said Florence. "I like having cousins."

"I've got a bit of news for you," said her father. "I've been saving it up for a long time. It wasn't only because of the frescoes that I stayed so long abroad. And some of the time I wasn't in Italy at all: I was in Paris. I went to talk to the art experts there, but I stayed for other reasons. Have you ever thought, Florence, I might be lonely too?"

"I suppose I have," said Florence. "When you were home, I've tried to be company for you. And I've tried to write letters—though I can't write long ones, somehow. Though I can talk a lot, in letters I run out of ideas."

Her father took her arm and tucked it into his own.

"Your letters are lovely," he said. "Dear Flo, you've always been good company to me. But I've met a lady—I met her in France—and I want her company, too. I mean, Florence, I'm going to be married again."

He and Florence stood still on the path; Florence thought how the clear pink roses, their petals edged with frost, looked crystallized.

"When?" she asked, her eyes fixed on the flowers.

"Soon after Christmas, I thought," said her father. "But you'll see her before that. In fact, Florence, you'll see her today. She's coming here to visit, on her way to London. I would have told you earlier, but I wanted to make sure you were strong enough for such a surprise."

"It is a surprise," said Florence slowly. "I think it's a nice one, though. If you like her, Daddy, I expect I shall like her too. She'll be my stepmother, though, won't she?"

"She will," said her father. "There are good stepmothers as well as wicked ones, Flo. She laughs a lot, and she's fun, and very, very kind. I really do think you'll like her."

"I don't think I'll call her Mother straight away," said

Florence. "I don't need to, do I? Could I call her aunt, or something?"

"You must ask her," said her father. "She'll be here this afternoon."

They started to walk again.

"What an exciting day," said Florence. "Shall we all live in the Paragon, after the wedding?"

"No—we'll leave the Paragon to the aunts," said her father. "I'm buying a new house, around the corner in the Square."

Florence felt great relief. Better if the new house had been even further away; but at least it would be a house where George had never been, where he might never be able to come.

"There's more to tell you," said her father. "One reason the Paragon won't be big enough is that the lady I'm marrying has a son. She's been a widow for a long time now, and she has a son of thirteen who can hardly remember his father. You'll have a brother, Florence."

"What are they called?" asked Florence, breathless. "What are they like, Daddy? Dark or fair?"

Her father laughed. "I'm not going to describe them, Florence," he said. "They'll be here so soon. My wife-to-be is called Marguerite Blanchard, and her son is called Louis."

"Those sound like French names," said Florence. "Are they French?"

"They have some French blood," said her father. "You'll learn perfect French from them, Florence. Especially Louis—he's been to school there."

Florence thought of a dark-skinned boy with a black, shining head; and her new pleasure turned into a creeping fear that raised goose pimples on her skin and made her teeth chatter.

"You're cold," said her father, and drew her back indoors.

It was a mercy that all the children except Florence were at school. The house that afternoon seemed all bustle and fuss. The two small attics were brought into instant use, though not really ready as bedrooms; Charles and Louis were to have one and Florence's father the other. Marguerite Blanchard was to have Charles's usual room, where Florence's father had been sleeping.

"I've no idea how long they're staying," Aunt Addy confided to Florence. "I do hope your new mother isn't too keen on things matching, Florence—nothing does. She's got a nice blue carpet, but the curtains are mainly brown and the bedspread's mainly green. They're so precise about everything in France."

"I don't know what she'll be like," said Florence, half distracted. "Or him. Louis. I wish I did."

"Oh, Louis," said Aunt Addy. "I'm not worrying about him. Boys are easy."

Florence silently thought that not all boys were as easy as Charles.

"And I've got no flowers," said Aunt Addy. "Run out, Florence, and see what you can find. There might be some of those little irises, and the winter jasmine's out. Find something—just a tiny spray—for Mrs. Blanchard."

Out in the garden, at the back of the house, Florence busied herself among the frosty flowers. The early dark was already coming when she heard carriage wheels, and thought her father must be driving off to the station to collect the Blanchards. But when she got back into the house, she heard animated voices; and in the hall was her father, newly back from the station, ushering in a tall woman in a black jacket over a green-and-black skirt, and a red-cheeked, lanky boy. The boy took off his flat cap and the woman took off her black hat, talking as she did so to Aunt Addy. Florence stood like a statue, staring. Marguerite and Louis had heads of flaming, glorious red hair (Marguerite's flat, and shining, Louis's standing up like a brush's bristles); and Marguerite's voice—soft and musical—had the unmistakable accent of the Scot.

"And here's my Florence," said her father. "With her hands full of flowers, as seems right. Come and shake hands, Florence, if you can manage it."

"The flowers are for you," said Florence, and began a curtsy, but Mrs. Blanchard pulled her into a hug and kissed her warmly.

"Florence," she said. "You're just like your mother—the picture in your father's locket. I shall feel I know her, too. And this is Louis. He's always wanted a brother or a sister—he'll be so happy to have you as his sister."

Louis first bowed politely, then unexpectedly kissed Florence. The kiss landed on the side of her nose; Florence blushed and Louis laughed.

"I shall get better with practice," he said. "I shall like having a sister. I hope you've been wanting a brother, because here I am."

"I've never thought," said Florence. "But perhaps I have. Perhaps it's just what I need."

13

Bellfield seemed to be an elastic house: It was almost as if it had stretched, effortlessly, to take in Marguerite and Louis Blanchard. After a day or two it seemed entirely natural to all the girls, not just Florence, to ask Marguerite for help with sewing, or to ask her to talk French to them or to tell them stories. Marguerite's stories soon became famous, especially her Scottish ghost stories. Crumbling castles and desolate moors, and the bagpipes mysteriously sounding when there was nobody alive in the house to play them, had all of the children and some of the adults sitting open-mouthed to listen. Marguerite found herself elevated to the rank of Favorite Aunt, called by everyone, even Florence, simply Marguerite. Aunt Addy made one attempt to get the children to address her more formally, but Marguerite squashed that herself.

"Being an auntie makes me feel too old," she said. "I think I'll be more of a sister. What's wrong with Marguerite as a name?"

"It's French," said Marcus, acting cheeky.

"And so was my grandfather French," said Marguerite. "And Louis's father was French on Sundays."

"What do you mean, French on Sundays?" demanded Ferdy.

"Never went to church," said Marguerite dramatically. "He said he preferred the French Sunday. He walked about in his best boots and ate too much."

"Ma and I went to church," said Louis. "Like good psalm-singing Scots. How shall we do for a church here, Ma? They'll be proper Anglicans and sing the psalms a different way."

"We shall do well enough, Louis," said his mother. "We shall go wherever our nice new family go."

"I'll sit by Florence, then," said Louis.

He didn't, in the event; when Sunday came he and Charles were already allies and sat together, exchanging bets on how many minutes the sermon would take and how many verses in the last hymn. Louis won, even though it was Charles's home territory. He seemed to be that kind of boy.

The Blanchards came to Bellfield in the first week of December. After a week, Florence's father left them there and went up alone to London. He had things to see to in the new house, and arrangements to make for the wedding.

"Don't you want to go with him?" Florence said to Marguerite.

"Well, a bit," said Marguerite. "Because it's him. I shall miss him. But he wants to get the house ready himself, and surprise me with it. Dear man! I do love surprises."

"But won't you care about what he does? Suppose he gets blue curtains, and you wanted green?" Florence asked.

"It'll be a long time before he gets to choosing curtains," said Marguerite. "I shan't mind, anyway. Odd, when you think I've moved in the world of art all my life; but I don't notice colors very much."

"Was your father an art historian too, then?" Florence asked Louis while Marguerite advised the other girls about some embroidery they were doing for their mother for Christmas.

"Yes; our fathers were friends," said Louis. "And when yours came to Paris, he came to see my ma to see how she was getting on and they fell in love."

"Aren't you pleased?" said Florence, feeling shy about asking him.

"Oh, fairly," said Louis. "I like your father, and Ma's going to be happy and she deserves it. And I've never known any girls so it's rather like studying a new species, having you and the cousins around."

It was certainly true that Louis watched Florence with interest. She was often aware of his eyes on her, and was prepared for anything she said to be met with a joking remark. At first Louis's teasing made her feel self-conscious; after a time she began not to notice it, or simply to tease him back. To provoke her he had only to call her "Sis," and he got quite a few cushions shied at his head on account of this. His second favorite among the girls was Nellie. Nellie accepted him as a new appendage of Florence's, lovable because Florence was loved; not handsome like Charles, but much funnier. She watched him as intently as he himself watched Florence.

Florence still kept on smuggling food out to the summerhouse, although it was difficult to do it under Louis's keen eyes. She still felt that George was around, not far off, and that the offering of food served in some way to keep him away from the house.

Once when a sugarcoated bun had been slid into Florence's roomy pocket, Louis—who was sitting beside her—raised his eyebrows at her and without a word cut his own bun in half and gave half to her.

"What are you doing, Louis?" said Audrey.

"Playing feed the lion," said Louis, unperturbed.

"What a pity it isn't summer and hay time—we could teach you lion hunt," said Audrey. "Florence was a lion then, too; but most of the time she was an antelope."

Florence shivered, thinking how she had met the bushbuck in the flowering grass.

She slipped away after tea, unbolted the garden door, and took to the summerhouse the sticky bun and two apples saved from a secret feast. It was already dark, and when she got back to the door she was shocked to see a boy standing there.

"George?" she asked tentatively, hanging back.

"It's me, Flo," said Louis's voice. "Before I let you back in the door—tell me, what lion have you been feeding?"

"What do you mean?" asked Florence, playing for time.

"Apples and a bun today; seedcake and a piece of cheese yesterday," said Louis. "I know where you put it—in the summerhouse. And I know who gets it."

"No, you don't," said Florence in anguish. "How can you?"

"I lay in wait to see who came," said Louis. "Twice. And I saw who came for it."

"Who, then?" said Florence, thinking she had better know the worst.

"Jacky from the stable yard," said Louis. "Both times, Jacky."

"But it can't have been!" exclaimed Florence. "It's a mistake. It can't be Jacky."

"Wrong lion, eh?" said Louis. "I don't know who it's meant for, Flo, or what the game is, but that's who's getting it. He scoffed it where he stood. I'd give the whole thing up if I were you."

"I shall have to," Florence later confided to Nellie. "If Louis knows I put out food, and he's seen Jacky taking it, there's no point going on."

"I don't think there ever was, Florence," said Nellie, whispering. "Food wouldn't stop George coming, because he never came for that. He came for you."

PART THREE

*Mid-December 1910 to Early April 1911
at the Paragon*

1

"How long are we going to stay at Bellfield?" Florence asked Marguerite one day. The two of them were alone by the drawing-room fire. Aunt Addy was in her own room "making Christmas arrangements," as she mysteriously put it. Charles and Louis had gone out with Uncle Crispin on his rounds, being allowed to take turns with the driving; this trip, on a raw and windy day, was thought too risky for Florence. For the other children, it was the next-to-last day of school.

"We've mainly been waiting for you to be well enough," said Marguerite. "You do seem stronger these last few days. Could you face the journey?"

"Oh yes, if I had you and Louis with me," said Florence. "But is our new house ready?"

"Far from it, I gather," said Marguerite, and laughed. "The plan is for your poor father to go on living in the new house and superintending the work. You and I and Louis will all stay at the Paragon for Christmas. The wedding is planned for early in the new year, and by then the new house ought to be liveable-in even if it's not perfect. Will you be my bridesmaid, Florence?"

"Oh yes, please, Marguerite; I should love that," said Florence. "But what shall I wear? Is my green dress nice enough?"

"You're to have a new dress—but it's a secret," said Marguerite. "You'll just have to be patient! How do you feel about leaving Bellfield?"

"Sad, in lots of ways," said Florence. "And I wish we were moving into our new house, not back to the Paragon."

"Don't you like the Paragon? Remember, I haven't seen it yet," said Marguerite.

"It's a haunted house," said Florence abruptly.

"Oh, is it?" said Marguerite. "Louis will like that. No, don't tell me about the ghost—I'm going to wait to be surprised. Not that it will get much of a look in, poor thing, with such a houseful. Louis is going to have to sleep in an attic again. Fortunately, he likes attics. Does the ghost haunt the attic?"

"It's been there," said Florence. "It's mostly in the garden."

"That makes it more of a summer ghost," said Marguerite. "Would you feel better about going back, Florence, if we took Nellie with us?"

"But we can't, Marguerite," said Florence. "She's got school, and this is her family."

"Suppose we borrowed her, just for Christmas?" said Marguerite.

"Would she want to come—and leave everybody here?" asked Florence.

"Well, ask her," said Marguerite. "And in case you should wonder, Florence, I can just as easily arrange for two bridesmaids' dresses."

*   *   *

Nellie, being asked, was enthusiastic both about spending Christmas in London and being a bridesmaid.

"They won't miss me here," she said to Florence. "There are such lots of us."

"Your mother will miss you," said Florence. "But she says you can come, so that's all right. I'd better tell Louis—I don't think anybody has."

"Will he mind?" said Nellie nervously. "I don't think he likes me much. Though he looks at me a lot."

"He's always watching," said Florence. "I don't see why he should mind, though. The Paragon isn't his home."

The next day, after breakfast, she separated Louis from Charles by telling Louis she had a message from his mother and taking him off to the shrubbery.

"What's this special message that can't be talked about indoors?" Louis demanded. "Dash it, Flo, be quick about it. We ought to have put our coats on—you'll get cold. Come on."

"It's just that Nellie's coming to London for Christmas," gabbled Florence. "Do you mind?"

"Mind!" exclaimed Louis, and patted Florence's shoulder. His eyes were bright.

"Don't tell anyone, Flo," he said. "Especially, don't tell her. But when we're all grown-up I'm going to marry Nellie. You can be my bridesmaid, too."

"You oughtn't to set your heart on it," said Florence, anxious for his feelings. "Aunt Addy may want her to marry somebody rich and great. She says Nellie's going to be beautiful."

"Nellie's beautiful now," said Louis. "And she's deep. You never know what Nellie's thinking, and when she says something it's a complete surprise. You're a bit like that, Flo, but I can't marry you; you're family."

Florence left Bellfield with her feelings in a whirl. There was all the regret of saying good-bye to her aunt and uncle and the cousins; to her surprise, and Audrey's, she cried over her parting with Audrey and had to borrow Louis's handkerchief. There was so much to look forward to, too: life with her father and Marguerite and Louis, which was bound to be fun; Nellie's visit (Nellie traveled back with them), and the wedding.

She was not sure how she felt about Louis making a third in her friendship with Nellie. She was not sure how she felt about sharing her new brother, even with Nellie; or sharing her father with both Blanchards. Fortunately there never seemed to be time to worry about these things.

Seeing the Paragon again, after so long, gave her a moment of dismay and fear. She looked up at the attic windows, as she and the other three piled out of the cab that had brought them from the station; she was afraid of seeing George's face there, pressed against the pane. There was nothing.

"Nice house," said Louis. "Here's your father coming, Flo. Yes—and the aunts!"

The aunts rose to the occasion as they rose to every occasion. It's true that they were somewhat startled by being kissed on both cheeks by Louis (at least, he reached James's cheek, but was nearer to the chin in Dorrit's case). But they seemed to like it.

"Delightful manners," said Dorrit, and James added, beaming, "How nice it will be to have a boy about the place! It will be quite like the old days, Theodore, when you came to stay as a boy."

Florence noticed Louis noticing this use of her father's first name, and smiled at Nellie.

Almost the first news her father had for them was about the new house, and it was bad. He broke it as they all ate tea.

"I got the feel from your letters that things weren't going well," Marguerite said to him. "Tell us the worst. Is it the title deeds?"

"Forged?" suggested Louis hopefully.

"No, no—there's nothing wrong with our title to the place," said Florence's father. "It's the actual fabric. The builders have found rot in the roof timbers; the whole of the roof will have to come off."

"Oh, my goodness!" said Marguerite. "And the worst weather of the year about to come upon us. January that brings the snow, and soaking February. What's the prospect—when might we be able to move in?"

"Easter," said Florence's father. His gloom was evident even through a mouthful of tea cake.

"So isn't it a happy chance," said Aunt James brightly, "that we've so much space in the Paragon and you can all live here as long as necessary?"

"But what an imposition on your kindness and hospitality!" Marguerite said. "All of us, for three months—when you'd expected us for three weeks!"

"It will be our pleasure," said Aunt Dorrit. "There will be room for you, too, Theodore, if you prefer."

"I'll stay in the Square for now," said Florence's father. "Until after the wedding, anyhow. But once they start actually removing the roof—well, we'll see."

"Heroic aunts to the rescue," said Louis. "But for you, we should all be in the streets, shivering in the snow."

Florence did shiver, thinking of the three months ahead in the Paragon.

There was no doubt that the aunts enjoyed the presence of Louis. Louis studied them carefully for a couple of days, and then said to Florence and Nellie, "I can see what they think. They think that *boys* means 'practical jokes.' So we shall have some."

"Us too?" asked Florence, and Nellie said, "I've never done a practical joke."

Thereafter a series of odd events broke out in the Paragon. Objects in bedrooms suddenly and jerkily moved at night (being attached to dark strands of cotton that disappeared under passage doors); spiders of hideous and sprawling immensity, made out of darning wool, dropped unexpectedly from curtains; odd sounds (often an imitation of the bagpipes) came startlingly from cupboards and from behind sofas. Florence, Nellie, Marguerite, and even the aunts all retaliated with tricks played on Louis, who regularly found holly in his boots and rotten apples in his coat pockets. Mrs. Peabody, with whom Louis was a bit of a favorite, forgot her dignity and joined in, serving him boiled string instead of spaghetti. In a house buzzing with secret activity, thought Florence, there would be no room at all for a real ghost.

Christmas was more fun than any Florence could

remember. Louis proved to be a great inventor of ridiculous games; Nellie proved to be one of those infectious gigglers who start a whole room shaking.

Marguerite's stories were enjoyed by firelight, while the company peeled oranges and cracked nuts; and the aunts dug in their memories and produced their own stories and riddles too.

"They were never like this when I was alone with them," Florence said to Nellie as they went to bed one night.

"Perhaps you were shy of them, so never got them started off," said Nellie. "Marguerite and Louis are the most unshy people I know. If they weren't so nice, they'd be awful. I'm so glad they'll be a bit of my family."

The wedding happened on a day of snow. Marguerite's dress was of aquamarine velvet, Florence's and Nellie's of a darker, greeny-blue. "A shallow sea and a deep sea," said Nellie. "We're the deep sea, Florence." The snowflakes settled on the velvet and on the white flowers that all three carried, and clung to the girls' hair. Florence was dazed with it all and never made an attempt to catch Marguerite's bouquet when she threw it; it landed in Nellie's hands and Louis gave Nellie a wink.

Theodore and Marguerite Wheatcroft went off for visits to Italy and Paris, to see their friends there, and life in the Paragon settled down, in spite of Louis's jokes. Louis was to start at a school near Florence's, in the hope that he would get a place in a boarding school for the following year, and he had some preparatory work to do. Florence worked over some of the things she had been doing when she left London, and Nellie amused herself.

The day before she was due to go back to Bellfield, Nellie came in in her outdoor coat and found Florence alone by the drawing-room fire. The aunts were at work and Louis was in his bit of the attic carving a wooden mouse.

Florence looked up idly, but saw at once that something was wrong. Nellie was unusually white, and her hands were gripped into fists.

"It's a good thing I'm going back tomorrow," she said. "I've just seen George."

"Where?" demanded Florence, dropping her book.

"In the street," said Nellie. "In the lane that goes down to the cemetery. I'd been for a walk and I was coming up the lane. He was on the other side of it, going down."

"What did he say?" asked Florence.

"He didn't say anything," said Nellie. "Just looked at me, and lifted his hat."

"He doesn't usually wear a hat," said Florence. "How did you know it was him?"

"From his photograph," said Nellie. "Not yours; one I found at Bellfield. I'm quite sure about it, Florence. And I felt—not scared, exactly, but very, very cold."

2

Uncle Crispin came to fetch Nellie, and she left with an invitation from the aunts to come back at Easter (echoed by Louis and Florence, in case the Wheatcrofts were in their own house by then). Louis and Florence both moped after she had gone, and were fractious with each other and the aunts for a day or two. Florence, moreover, looked over her shoulder every time she went indoors, and took to bolting her bedroom door at night. The empty camp bed that had been Nellie's, standing beside her own, made her feel all the more lonely and vulnerable.

School soon distracted them both from their glooms. The school Louis went to was the brother school of Florence's, and in the next street; so she had his company on the way there every day. Sometimes they came back at different times, because of Florence's dancing and piano lessons and Louis's team practices and choir practices and such; but sometimes a cheerful gang made up of Florence, Barbara, Winnie, Louis, Reggie, and Dick came chattering home together.

Florence realized as soon as school began that Louis was a social asset. He was a very fast runner, and so in great demand for games; and his lively good humor and continual patter of jokes made him popular with everyone—except his teachers, who complained of the perpetual bubbling-up of laughter in his corner of the classroom. Even they couldn't complain about his work. He was brilliant at nothing, except French, where he had an unnatural advantage, and—for no apparent reason—history; but he was competent at everything. Florence, struggling to make up the lost weeks of lessons, envied his calm assurance and openly picked his brains. Her French homework improved beyond description.

When Valentine's Day came, a shoal of valentines arrived for Louis—some romantic and some comic. (One comic one was from Mrs. Peabody.) The aunts were highly amused.

"It must be that people like a fellow who makes them laugh," he said. "Nobody could say I'm handsome, could they?"

"Not now," said Dorrit. "I have a feeling you may be quite a presentable man, when your face fills out and your hair lies down—if it ever does."

"Your mother's a fine-looking woman," added James.

Florence contributed nothing to this. She was staring, tense with shock, at her third valentine. One was unsigned, and she suspected it came from Reggie. One was a comic one, from Louis, and signed "Your doting bro." The third was a pretty one, with lilies of the valley on the front, a silver ribbon, and a frill of silver lace; it was signed, in firm round handwriting and very black ink, "George."

"Are you all right, Florence?" asked Aunt Dorrit.

"Yes, thank you, Aunt," said Florence mechanically. But she could eat or drink no more breakfast and she was silent on the way to school. Winnie asked if the cat had got her tongue, and Barbara said she must be in love.

At the end of the school day Louis met her at her school gates. "I'm seeing you home, Flo," he said.

"You can't," said Florence. "I've got a music lesson."

"That's all right," said Louis. "I'll wait for you." And all through Florence's piano lesson he sat in the narrow hallway of the house of Mrs. Barber, who taught her, with his school cap on his knees. It was too dark there to read and he sat in patient silence, listening to Florence's inexpert fingering and Mrs. Barber's frequent remarks of "Expression, Florence!" and "Pedal!"

The two of them walked home in silence, and found they were to have tea on their own—the aunts had gone around to the Square, where a dining-room carpet was being laid in the new house. Louis ate enough for two and Florence hardly anything. At the end of tea he said, "Come up to my room," and towed her up the two flights of stairs to his attic. It had been a bright day, and the room was still warm with the remembrance of the February sun.

"Sit on the bed," said Louis. "And I'll sit by you. What I'm short of up here is chairs—we'd be all right if you could sit on pictures." There were plenty of pictures (Aunt James's), stacked or leaning against the wall.

"What's all this for?" asked Florence restlessly.

"It's for me to apologize," said Louis. "I'm sorry I've upset you, and I didn't mean to."

"What have you done?" said Florence. "Louis—not the card?"

"I'm afraid so, Florence," said Louis. "It was from me. I only meant to tease; I didn't realize you'd really mind."

Florence burst into tears that came from a mixture of anger and relief, cried tempestuously for five minutes, and then became aware of an overwhelming curiosity.

"But what do you know about George; and how?" she asked.

"I heard you and Nellie talking," said Louis. "But first—remember?—you called me George at Bellfield, at the garden door. And I thought George must be the person the food was meant for. I listened out after that for anything about George. Nosy is my middle name."

"What did you hear us say?" asked Florence.

"Only odd bits," said Louis. "I thought it was a story you two had made up. You and Nellie are marvelous at inventing things; I wish I was as good. It wasn't till today, when I saw you were upset by the card, that I remembered you thought this house was haunted. Ma told me that. And now, Flo, you've got to tell me everything. I won't have you creeping about half scared all the time."

"I don't know what you can do," said Florence, sounding as dreary as she felt. "You're only a boy." All the same, she told Louis the whole story—more than she had ever told, even to Nellie. The photograph and the knife; the circle of stones; the night games and Mr. Creed; George's appearance at Bellfield and her fall; her throwing of the knife into the well, and the finding and losing of the drowned boy; and the visit to the wood when she nearly died.

"I'll tell you the truth, Florence," said Louis at the end of this recital. "You've got too much imagination. You invented George."

"I didn't, Louis," whispered Florence, her tears beginning again.

"You were lonely, and you wanted a person to play

with," said Louis. "So you imagined somebody, and you imagined so hard you made him seem real."

"He didn't go away when I stopped wanting him," Florence pointed out.

"Your imagination's too strong for you. It runs away with the rest of your mind," insisted Louis.

"But Nellie saw him too. The day before she went home," said Florence.

Louis hesitated, as if shaken. "She's as bad as you are, then," he said at last. "Was the George she saw exactly the same as yours?"

"I don't know for sure," said Florence. "He was wearing a hat. Mine doesn't usually."

"There you are, then," said Louis. "You're to stop worrying, Florence. I'm here now and I reckon I'm a match for any George. If you see him, shout for me."

"All right," said Florence. "But I do hope I don't see him, Louis. I never want to see him again."

"Then you won't," said Louis soothingly. "I can hear the aunts. You'd better tidy up; I'll go down and talk to them."

He said no more about the incident to Florence. But next day he managed to be alone in the kitchen with Mrs. Peabody, ostensibly to scrape the bowls for the remnants of her cake and pudding mixtures. Mrs. Peabody, always glad to have somebody to gossip to when Hannah was not around, was talking about her troubles with the fishmonger. Louis abruptly interrupted her.

"Please, Mrs. Peabody," he said. "Will you clear up a mystery for me—I know you can. It's to do with Florence, and what I think has been upsetting her. Who was Georges Valery?"

143

3

The later part of February that year was all wind and rain, and day after day Florence and Louis came in wet and chilled from a journey home through puddles and squalls. Marguerite and Florence's father came home from abroad complaining dramatically about the English climate; and the house in the Square slowly got its new roof—though some days weren't fit for outdoor labor and the builders went off to work somewhere warmer.

Nothing was said about George until one Saturday when Louis and Florence were up in Louis's attic. They had a kerosene heater, and had been instructed to stay indoors—they had both had colds, and had what Marguerite called rusty chests.

"Drawing paper!" said Florence, ferreting around among Louis's property inside a large tin trunk. "Can I draw, Louis?"

"Yes—and give me a piece. I'll draw, too," said Louis. "I'll do a storm at sea. What will you do?"

"I want something to copy," said Florence. "I'll have a hunt through Aunt James's pictures and find an easy one to do."

"I'll have a look, too," said Louis, and together they turned the piles of canvases over and around and hunted through.

"Crumbs!" said Louis, gazing at an especially leafy wreath of rosebuds and clematis. "Copy this, Florence— I dare you. Aunt James is such an old dear, I wish she did something a bit better than this."

"But it's pretty," said Florence. "So's this one, with the butterflies. There's a kitten here somewhere, with a blue bow."

"Marshmallows," said Louis. "It's true they're pretty, but they're not real."

"Why not?" said Florence. "Rosebuds do look like that."

"A few; but in a big bunch of rosebuds some would have caterpillars on and some would be battered around the edges," said Louis. "She never paints that. She doesn't paint the truth."

"How funny," said Florence. "That's just what George said. He said it wasn't good art, hers or Aunt Dorrit's. I didn't understand what he meant."

There was a silence between them, Louis thinking, I hope she doesn't see the significance of that, and Florence thinking, but—but . . .

At last she said aloud, with painful slowness, "If I invented George, Louis, how can he have opinions I don't agree with? And ideas I've never had?"

"Perhaps you have ideas you aren't really aware of, Florence," said Louis. "People do. Or dreams. You might have thought those things in a dream and forgotten them when you woke up."

"Perhaps," said Florence. "But I don't think I did, Louis. Let's go down and see if Marguerite and Daddy are in, or the aunts. I don't want to draw, after all."

"Does Hannah have a young man?" said Florence's father to Aunt Dorrit a few weeks later. "Several times when I've come back to the house I've seen a young man near the back gate. A rather smart one, too; though I didn't see him really close."

"Dear me," said Aunt Dorrit. "I don't know of any young man, but I suppose I'd better ask her. If she's walking out I'll see about letting her invite him in once a week, if Mrs. Peabody doesn't object."

"I know the young man you mean, ma'am," said Mrs. Peabody when Dorrit did speak to her. "Least, I've seen him; I don't know who he is, and Hannah's never noticed him; I asked her. He looks as if he was making up his mind to something—like knocking maybe to ask for work. I feel I've seen him before, but I can't think where."

"Oh, surely not, Dorrit," Florence's father said when Aunt Dorrit repeated this conversation to him. "He looks too nicely dressed and groomed to be looking for odd jobs. If he keeps on hanging around, I'll notify the police."

Mr. Wheatcroft never did notify the police, but he kept a watch on the back gate himself. The loiterer did not appear at the gate again, but Mrs. Peabody said she had seen him elsewhere in the neighborhood, "wearing out his shoe leather doing nothing," as she put it.

"We can't concern ourselves with the whole of London," said Marguerite when she heard this. "If he's not around our back gate he's doing no harm to us; so let it go."

Louis listened to all this attentively, and did his own share of fruitless watching.

Nellie got permission to come to London for a fortnight at Easter, and grand preparations were made for her arrival. Florence decorated Nellie's bed with paper flowers, made from last Christmas's wrapping paper, and put a bunch of primroses on her bedside table; Louis put his wooden mouse inside the bed—Nellie hadn't seen it yet and, "She'll like a surprise," he said.

"We ought to be in the new house," Florence said to him as they stood looking at the bed. "There's lots more room there; Nellie could have her own room."

"She likes sharing yours," said Louis. "The two of you will be giggling up to midnight tonight. Ma says the new house will be ready about the time Nellie goes, so this will be our last holiday in the Paragon."

"It sounds sad, but I'm not really sorry," said Florence. "You know why, Louis."

"Yes, I know," Louis said.

Nellie's first day in London was all talk and laughter, and her scream at seeing Louis's mouse was loud enough to satisfy even him (as he lurked in the passage outside the bedroom door). As she wanted immediate revenge on him, the day ended with hurled pillows and Louis had to barricade himself in the attic.

But trouble followed close after this happy beginning. Louis and the two girls went out next day to bowl hoops in the park; and Nellie had hardly got the hang of her borrowed hoop before she suddenly stopped dead and let it fall. Florence, looking over her shoulder to see where Nellie had got to, was puzzled to see her standing on the path, staring at the shrubbery nearby.

Florence caught her own hoop and ran back. "What's the matter?" she asked, and Nellie pointed into the bushes.

"He was there," she said. "He looked out at me and smiled; then he went into the taller trees and I lost sight of him."

"Call Louis," said Florence, and shouted herself.

Louis, who was ahead, came careering back and began at once to search among the bushes. There was no sign of anybody except a badly behaved dog whose owner was whistling pointlessly on the other side of the park.

"Give it up," said Nellie finally. "Let's go on. I did see him, though."

She picked up her hoop and started off up the path, followed by the others. They threw themselves energetically into hoop rolling, but they all felt tense and oppressed. The glitter had gone off the day.

That night, Nellie slept badly and Florence from time to time woke and heard her moving restlessly in bed. In the morning Nellie looked white and exhausted, and Marguerite suggested that she should stay at home with the aunts while the others went to church. Nellie accepted this gladly.

The church-going party returned, Florence subdued and Louis silent, to find that Nellie was not with the aunts. The two of them ran upstairs to the girls' bedroom, and found Nellie there; she was sitting on her bed hugging her knees, and she had been crying.

"Nellie—" began Florence, going to her; but Louis pulled her back and interrupted her.

"Have you seen him again?" he said.

Nellie nodded. "I just went out to walk around the garden," she said. "It's such a lovely day. And suddenly there he was, looking over the back gate. I ran straight back indoors; but I heard him call me. He said 'Nellie.'"

"Have you quarreled with Nellie?" Marguerite asked Florence that afternoon. "Or has Louis?"

"No," said Florence, "Why?"

"She looks upset," said Marguerite. "The aunts noticed it too. They said she looked haunted, and that it was how you used to look before you went to Bellfield."

"I think she's having bad dreams," said Florence. "Marguerite—you know I said this was a haunted house."

"Yes?" said Marguerite. "Are you saying Nellie dreams ghosts? Is that what you used to do?"

"Something like that," said Florence. "But one ghost, Marguerite."

"I nearly told her," she said later to Louis. "I wonder if she'd understand? My father didn't."

"She probably would," said Louis. "Florence, tonight—put your bed very close to Nellie's, and leave a night-light burning."

4

That night, Nellie slept more calmly. But early in the morning, as the gray light overwhelmed the night-light's glow, Florence woke and saw her standing at the window, staring down into the garden.

Florence went to her, and put her arms around her. Nellie was icy cold.

"Is he there?" whispered Florence, and as Nellie didn't answer she went and looked out. The garden lay white with dew in the early, colorless quiet, and it was empty.

Florence pulled Nellie into her own bed and cuddled her into warmth and speech.

"He called me again, Florence," Nellie said. "He was in the garden. I felt I had to go down, but I resisted; I wouldn't go. I can't go on fighting it. I wonder if I ought to go back to Bellfield."

"He came to Bellfield after me," Florence reminded her, and Nellie shivered.

"We'll do something," Florence promised her. "I'll talk to Louis."

Marguerite came to their room at getting-up time, and said that Nellie should have breakfast in bed. Nellie was unwilling, feeling that she would rather be with Florence, but Marguerite was at her firmest.

Immediately after breakfast Florence took Louis to one side. "We've got to talk," she said.

"My room, then," said Louis; and the two settled up there.

"Council of war," said Florence, using the phrase Charles used to like. "George came into the garden, this time, and he called her to go down. It was early this morning. He used to call me like that, and I used to go. Nellie's stronger than me, I think; but if we don't do something, she'll go in the end."

"Yes," said Louis. "And you nearly died."

"You think Nellie might die!" whispered Florence. "Nellie!"

"How do I know? But she's in danger," said Louis. "You've got to stop it, Florence."

"Me!" said Florence. "How can I?"

"You began it—you called George," said Louis. "It's up to you to make him go."

"I nearly did, once," said Florence. "I threw his knife in the well."

"But when you saw him drowned, you felt sorry; and so he came back," said Louis.

"I don't know," said Florence. "Maybe. But what can I do? I don't know the truth about him, Louis. I hardly know more than his name."

"Didn't you ask?" said Louis. "Ask the family?"

"Yes, but nobody would tell me," said Florence. "Remember, they thought I was in a funny state, ill, and sleepwalking. I asked the aunts, and they said I should ask Daddy. I asked him, and he didn't tell me anything."

"I made Mrs. Peabody tell me," said Louis. "And I'll tell you."

"I'm not sure I want to know," said Florence.

"That's just the trouble," said Louis, cross now. "You'll have to know, if you're to do anything."

"All right," said Florence. "Go on."

"Aunt Dorrit and Aunt James had two sisters," Louis said. "One was the eldest of the four and one was the youngest. The youngest married your grandfather."

"I know that," said Florence. "They went to China."

"The eldest disgraced herself—or so some people thought," said Louis. "She ran away from home and married a Frenchman, called Maurice Valery. Georges was their son."

"Then what relation would he be to me?" asked Florence. "My grandmother's nephew—it sounds like an uncle, or something. I'm sure he's not my uncle!"

"No, not an uncle—a cousin," said Louis. "A third cousin, I think. But I don't understand family trees."

"He's about as old as me, in his photograph," said Florence. But she realized as she said it that she had no idea how old the photograph was.

Louis hurried on. "The other thing about him, Flo," he said, "was that he wanted to run off with your mother. While she was engaged to your father, and when she was visiting the aunts, Georges came over to London. He came to see the aunts and he fell for Lily. He tried to get her to break her engagement and elope with him. The aunts knew he had a bad reputation, and they got your father to come; and all together, they drove him away. He hated both your parents, after that."

152

"Why did he have a bad reputation?" Florence asked.

"He was a bad lot," Louis said. "He was a gambler, and stories were told that when he'd gambled all his own money away he cheated other people out of theirs, or stole it off them. Girls liked him, especially young ones, and some fell in love with him; but he ditched them when he lost interest. One drowned herself when he left her."

"Drowned herself!" Florence exclaimed.

"Well, she was found drowned," said Louis. "Her brother had been killed in a fight, and although it was never proved, people suspected that the other person in the fight was George. And funnily enough, George himself died by drowning. Not here, but in France, and in a river. His body had stab wounds in it, although it wasn't from those that he died—the river killed him. His death is still a mystery."

"They ought to have told me all that," said Florence. "The aunts. If they had, I wouldn't have wanted him to come."

"One other thing Mrs. Peabody told me," said Louis. "She said he was always a very lonely and unhappy man. If a ghost did walk, it might be out of loneliness."

"George walks, if you can call it that, because I sent for him," said Florence. "I called him, Louis. But it's like 'The Sorcerer's Apprentice' and all those folk stories. When you start something, you don't realize you can't stop it; and what's more, it will grow—it will get powerful."

After a silence, Louis went on, "He's buried here, Florence. He had no family in France; his parents were both dead. The aunts and your father had him brought to England, and he's buried in the cemetery here."

"In our cemetery!" exclaimed Florence. "Just down the lane! Louis, he's almost on our doorstep. And Nellie is seeing him."

"Only you can save Nellie," Louis said. "You started it, and you must be the one to stop it."

"But can I?" asked Florence.

"Yes, you can," said Louis. "This isn't a fairy story. And you have the strength. You're a strong person, Florence. If you weren't, you would have died that night, when you dreamed that nightmare about the wood."

5

Louis's words were with Florence all day. *Only you can save Nellie; only you* . . . Nobody but me, said Florence to herself. And I must; whatever it means.

But it could mean only one thing. She would herself go out to George, knowing that she might not come back.

It never occurred to her to call George in full daylight. George belonged to the dark hours. Darkness would make it all—what had to happen—more bearable, less real.

As soon as twilight came, Florence began her preparations. Mr. Creed had gone home. She brought from the house George's photograph and the silver knife; she picked another basketful of white stones from the border edges and she made a circle as before. Not such a neat, tight circle this time; hurry and fear drove her, and the circle straggled and had gaps. But it would do.

She was too early for real darkness, but she decided not to wait. In the gray light, she stood in her circle and called George.

"Please come, George," she said. "I know I said I didn't want you; but now I do. And this time I'll do what you want. I'll go with you."

"Of course," said a mocking voice, and Florence had to

shut her teeth on a scream. Standing not in her circle, but close to it, was somebody. Not the young George in his dark blue jersey, but a man. Even in that poor light Florence felt sure this was somebody she had seen before: dark-eyed, dark-haired, nattily dressed with a wing collar and a curly-brimmed bowler hat. She had seem him, she thought, somewhere in the neighboring streets.

Her voice seemed to have gone, and she could only whisper, "Who are you?"

"Georges, of course," said the man. "Who else?"

"George is a boy," Florence whispered.

"Yours may have been," said the man. "Nellie's isn't. Why didn't you ever ask her?"

"I never thought," said Florence. "Perhaps I was afraid to think."

The man only smiled, and in that smile Florence recognized her George, George the boy.

"I want all this to end, George," she said—with more voice now. "I want it to end, however it ends. I said I'd do what you want, and I will."

"What, be my blood sister?" said George, grinning.

"If that's what you want," said Florence.

"Not anymore," said George. "That was what young George in his secret wood would have done. Not what I'd do."

"Don't you want me, then?" asked Florence.

"Oh, yes," said George. "But I want Nellie, too."

"No," said Florence.

"Yes," said George. "Come to the park, in the morning. As soon as it's light. Both of you, in your bridesmaid's dresses. I liked those."

"But how—" Florence began.

"I was in the church," said George. "Nobody saw me, because nobody wanted to see me. And all churches have dark places at the back, and behind pillars."

"I won't bring Nellie," Florence said, but she said it to the air. She was alone in the nearly dark garden.

Most of that night, Florence sat in her bed, or lay against humped-up pillows, watching while Nellie slept. Nellie slept lightly, with uneasy dreams. Sometimes she moaned and twice she said, "No, no," in nightmares. Florence touched her without waking her, when this happened; and Nellie settled into deeper sleep.

Toward morning Nellie's bad dreams seemed to have gone, and she was sleeping peacefully. Florence got up as soon as the light strengthened, and put on her bridesmaid's dress. She was not going to go into the mud of the park in white stockings and wedding slippers, so her weekday socks and school boots had to do. She wanted—irrationally, but strongly—something of Nellie's with her and she took from the hall Nellie's dark-blue hooded cloak. She went down the garden path in stockinged feet and put the boots on at the gate.

The streets were almost empty and Florence saw nobody close to—only a hurrying figure or two in the distance. The park gates, which she had expected to find locked, mysteriously opened to her push. Had George come first and picked the lock, she wondered? But did George need to open gates?

George the man met her on a path near the gates, where he stood waiting for her. Birds were beginning to sing in the gray air and dew lay heavy and white on the grass. It was, Florence thought—in the middle of her fear and her sense of hopeless inevitability—a perfect morning.

"Why haven't you brought Nellie?" said George.

"She's too ill to come," said Florence.

"Then I shall have to go back for her," said George.

"No," said Florence. "It's a bargain. You can have me but you don't get Nellie. And if you don't agree, I won't stay."

George's eyebrows rose. "And do I keep bargains? Me?" he said.

"I don't know," said Florence. "You never made one."

"I never did. And I never failed," said George. "I'm not the Outlandish Knight, Florence. You needn't think so."

"I don't think so," said Florence. She knew well enough that she had no hope of dragging George underwater.

"All right, we make a bargain," said George. "My first! I won't go back for Nellie. And you do whatever I say."

"You know I will," said Florence. She wondered if in fact she had any choice. This George would be too fast to run from.

"Come down to the water," said George, and Florence walked with him to the edge of the lake. The ducks were standing on the bank, heads tucked in, still half asleep.

"It's not deep enough," said Florence, looking at the dark water.

"It will do," said George. "Wade out a bit."

Remembering that it was Nellie's, Florence flung the cloak over a bush, took off her boots, and waded slowly into the water. The mud was thick and squelchy and her progress was clumsy; the soaked velvet clung around her knees. George was not beside her and she heard no swish of the water behind; but she expected at any moment a push that would send her facedown into the ooze.

She was waist-deep before any touch came; and then it was a hand on her shoulder and a voice saying quietly, "Flo!"

She swung around, blank-faced, to see Louis just behind her in his shirtsleeves. There was no sign of George.

"You must go back, Louis," said Florence, softly. "He agreed. If I did what he wanted, he wouldn't go back for Nellie."

Horror and comprehension dawned in Louis's face. "But you can't do this, Flo!" he said. "You can't do it. It's mad."

"You said only I could save her," said Florence.

"But I didn't mean by sacrificing yourself," said Louis. "How could I? How could I have meant that?"

"You want to marry Nellie," said Florence, like somebody reasoning with an obstinate child. "You care about her. You said I was to save her."

"But not like this, for heaven's sake!" Louis burst out. "Florence—you're my sister. Don't you know you matter too?"

"What did you mean, then?" said Florence, cold and exhaustion combining to induce a sense of stupidity and futility.

"Make him go back. Bell, book, and candle," Louis said. "Before he gets any more powerful."

"When did he disappear?" said Florence. "I thought any minute he would push me under."

"There wasn't anybody," said Louis. And to her shocked disbelief: "Really, Florence. I didn't see anyone but you. You were wading out on your own."

"It would have saved Nellie," said Florence.

"Not necessarily," said Louis. "Promises, piecrust. Not everybody keeps promises."

"I believed him," said Florence. "It would have worked, Louis. Why did you come?"

"I had a nightmare," said Louis. "That you were walking in your sleep, and were in danger. So I got up and dressed and sat on the attic stairs to watch your door. I was behind you all the way. I'd have stopped you from going into the lake, only I got stuck at the gates. They seemed to be locked, and I had to climb over. I don't know how you got in."

"You should have let me alone," said Florence.

"And how should we have been any better off, if Nellie had died of grief?" asked Louis sharply.

In utter dreariness, Florence began to cry; and Louis took her arm and steered her step by step out of the water, to where Nellie's cloak and his coat and two pairs of boots waited on the water's edge.

"My dress will be spoiled," said Florence, as Louis hauled her out.

"Good velvet washes," said Louis. "And that's the best. I chose it."

"Did you?" said Florence. "Why?"

"Ma's got no sense of color. She took me along," said Louis. "It's a lovely color. Water color."

"Yes," said Florence, and looked back briefly over the empty gray lake.

6

Mrs. Peabody and Hannah were up when Florence and Louis got back, and Louis managed to convince them that Florence had gone out for an early walk and slid into the water down a muddy bank, and that he had got wet pulling her out. It might be harder, of course, to convince the aunts.

Florence and Louis sat in the kitchen, drinking hot milk and wrapped in blankets, while water was heated for baths for them.

"We've got to try again, then," Florence said, sounding determined but hopeless. "What shall we do?"

"You know as well as I do," said Louis. "You called him. But I think we should go to his grave."

"Do you know where it is?" said Florence. "I know the cemetery's only just down the lane; but I think it's very large and wandery."

"Yes, I've seen it," said Louis. "The aunts told me where to look."

"I must take his things," said Florence. "The knife, and his photograph."

"Nellie's photograph of him, too, if you can get it," said Louis.

"And some of the white stones, to make a circle," said

Florence. "They're still on the garden path, Louis. I put them out last night."

"I'll get them," said Louis. "When shall we go?"

"After breakfast," Florence said. "Before Nellie gets up. She mustn't know, Louis. She isn't safe."

Florence had to go into her bedroom, to get dry clothes and to fetch the photographs and the knife. Nellie's breakfast tray stood on the floor, tea finished but toast no more than nibbled. Nellie had rolled herself in her bedclothes and was fast asleep.

Florence set herself a time limit for finding Nellie's photograph: If she hadn't discovered it in five minutes, she would give up. The bedroom clock ticked heavily while she tried the obvious places: purse, underclothes drawer, handkerchief pile. She thought last of books, and looked at the heap on the floor by Nellie's bed. *English Ballads* was at the bottom. Florence slid it out and riffled through the pages. The photograph was in it, marking the page of "The Outlandish Knight." The adult George's smile mocked under his dashing bowler; and on either side of it Florence read:

An outlandish knight from the north land came,
And he came wooing of me. . . .

"For six pretty maids I've drowned here before,
And the seventh thou art to be.

Pull off, pull off your silken gown,
And deliver it unto me,

For I think it's too fine and much too gay
To rot in the saltwater sea. . . ."

With her fingers shaking she took the photograph, returned the book, picked up her own photograph and the knife, and silently turned the door handle.

By the time Florence got downstairs again, Louis was in coat, boots, scarf, and cap and had already told the aunts (not being able to find his mother) that he and Florence were going out.

"Where did you say we were going?" Florence muttered as the front door shut behind them.

"To get Nellie a cheering-up present," said Louis. "We can do that afterward. Hang on a moment—I've got to pick up the stones, and get something from Mr. Creed."

Florence was mystified by this, and was still mystified when Louis came back carrying a trowel and a garden basket containing not only white stones, but also pansies in pots.

"You'll see what they're for," he said, forestalling her questions. "I'll pay for them out of my pocket money, so it's all right."

The steep little road down to the cemetery was empty of people, and there was nobody to wonder about a girl and a boy running down it carrying between them a load of bouncing flowerpots.

Florence pulled Louis to a walk before they reached the gates.

"Slow down," she said. "There's a sort of keeper. I've seen him."

"I know," said Louis.

The gates, opening off the lane, were huge and of iron, set in stone arches. There were ponderous entrance buildings, including chapels and an office. The cemetery stretched into the distance but Louis seemed to know where he was going. He led the way firmly through the gates.

Although Louis and Florence were quiet, and felt they were completely insignificant, they were noticed. A dark-suited man came out of the office and called after them.

Florence guessed at once that boys were not popular in the cemetery; she also realized what the pansies were for.

"We've come with some flowers," she said politely. "For our cousin's grave."

"Who's your cousin?" asked the man, not in an unfriendly way.

"Georges Valery," said Florence.

"We can find it all right," said Louis. He held the pansies well forward so that the man could not avoid seeing them.

"All right," he said. "Let me know when you leave. I'll be in here."

Shortly after Florence and Louis, a well-dressed dark man spoke to the official at the gate—and followed them in.

"Can we run again?" whispered Florence.

"Better not," said Louis. "If there are any gardeners about, they might think it was unsuitable behavior."

"I've never been in here before—isn't that odd," said Florence. "The aunts never brought me here, and the other girls don't like it. Daddy and I always walked in the park. I suppose my mother's here."

"Is she?" said Louis. "That's a nice idea."

"It's huge, this place," said Florence. "Do you really know the way? It's funny, isn't it—it doesn't seem a sad place. If I'd known that, I'd have come before."

"Jolly interesting," said Louis. "There's a stone dog on one of these graves. And somewhere there's a stone lion."

"What are the buildings down the flights of steps?" asked Florence.

"Vaults for bones," said Louis. "There are some above-ground vaults too. One day we'll come here to explore."

"How many graves?" asked Florence.

"No idea," said Louis. "It looks like thousands and thousands."

They did pass a gardener as they went along; but he too seemed to accept the pansies and the trowel as an adequate entrance ticket.

Most of the time they walked in silence, until at last Louis said, "This is the one."

It was a plain grave, with a simple cross, and a rose-bush growing in the middle of its mound. On the arms of the cross was carved GEORGES VALERY, and on the shaft below AGED 41; but there were no dates of birth and death.

"Forty-one!" said Florence.

"Don't think," said Louis. "We've got a job to do. We'll plant the pansies first, because that's our alibi."

He dug energetically with the trowel, and set the pansies into the soil around the base of the rosebush. Toward the head of the grave, he loosened some soil but didn't plant the last of the pansies.

"You must do the last bit," he said to Florence. "You know what to say."

Florence squatted, and dug a small, deep hole where Louis had softened up the earth for her. She surrounded it with a circle of white stones, and pulled from her pocket the two rather crumpled photographs and the bright knife.

As her hand went out toward the hole, holding them, a scream sounded from higher up in the cemetery.

"No! No!" said the screaming voice; and then, on a long-drawn-out cry, "Florence!" It was Nellie's voice.

"Don't stop," said Louis. "I'll go. Whatever happens, Florence, don't stop what you're doing. You must finish it. Finish it."

While he ran, Florence clenched her teeth. The photographs and the knife went into the hole; the last of the pansies was planted above them. Then she stood up and said, as clear as she knew how, "You are to go, George. Go. You don't belong with us. Go back where you ought to be. Go. Go. Go. And this time, don't come again." She filled in the hole with loose earth and trod it down.

Nothing happened, and Florence's courage dropped like a stone. There was no token of George's going. She had seen him come; what did it mean, if she didn't see him go?

All the same, there was no more she could do. She

picked up the trowel and the basket and ran in the direction that Louis had gone.

She expected to have difficulty in finding him; in fact she nearly fell over him. At the top of a steep flight of steps that went down into a vault, Louis was kneeling. By him lay the body of Nellie, her long hair tumbled and her face a green-tinged white.

"Is she dead?" asked Florence, kneeling too.

"No," said Louis. "She's breathing. Rub her hands, Florence. I wish we had some water."

Florence had seen a watering can nearby, standing by a little box bush. She ran for that, and poured some muddy-looking water over Nellie's hands.

Louis rubbed Nellie's face with a moistened handkerchief, and Florence rubbed her wet hands. After a few minutes Nellie opened her eyes and stared at them.

"Where did he go?" she said.

"Now don't try and talk, Nellie," said Florence, fussing.

"It's all right," said Nellie. "I haven't hit my head or broken any legs. And he's gone, hasn't he?" She sat up and Louis patted her back.

"Yes, he's gone," he said. "At least, if Florence finished what she was doing."

"I did," said Florence. "But nothing happened. I wanted to see him go."

"That's because he was here," said Nellie. "I saw him go."

"Tell us," said Louis. "How did you come to be here?"

"I woke up when the front door shut," said Nellie. "I

looked out of the bedroom window and I saw Louis with the trowel and the plants. I knew you would be coming here and what for. I wanted to be part of it."

"So you followed us," said Louis.

"Yes," said Nellie. "I didn't realize I wouldn't be able to catch up with you, and that I'd lose sight of you. I didn't know which part of the cemetery you'd gone to but the man at the gate told me which way to start off. I thought I'd never find you. Then I saw George. He was coming after me. I ought to have shouted then, but I couldn't think; so I began to run."

"And did you fall?" asked Florence.

"When I got to the top of these steps, I looked around, and he was just behind me," said Nellie. "His arm was out and I knew he meant to push me down the steps. I screamed for you. He was between me and the sun and he looked sort of blurry; but he was real. We froze like that, just looking at each other, and then he vanished. Just disappeared—and there was nothing but the light there."

"So he did really go," said Florence, satisfied.

Louis said nothing. He was looking down the long flight of stone stairs ending in a door that looked as if it was made out of stone itself.

7

They went home the long way around, through the park; all arm in arm, with Nellie in the middle. Florence and Nellie both looked gray and tired but not, Louis thought, haunted.

"We shan't ever understand all of it," said Florence as they paused at a steep bit and looked back over their shoulders toward the quiet cemetery. "When we're all married, and tell stories to our children, do you think we shall even believe it?"

"Why not?" said Louis, teasing. "Since you invented it!"

"There was a dead boy in the well at Bellfield," said Florence doggedly.

"True enough," said Louis, his expression changing. "All right: We shall never understand it. That bit, anyway."

"Poor George," said Nellie unexpectedly.

"Why 'poor George'?" asked Florence, her eyebrows raised.

"Dragged here because you wanted him—and then you didn't," said Nellie. "And sent away because none of us want him—because we've got our own lives to lead; because the idea of him is frightening. Do you suppose his life was always like that?"

"Mrs. Peabody said he was always lonely," said Florence. "So I suppose he is 'poor George.' I think I was lonely before you two came along. And then there you were—and Louis made me fight George, and Nellie made me want to."

"I didn't do anything," said Nellie. "You both had to do things for me."

"Yes, you did," said Florence. "Even before we talked to each other, at Bellfield, you were somehow on my side. You were interested in me and my secrets—that mattered. And you opened the garden door for me."

"Let's drop the subject," said Louis. "Let's go and make sure Mother and everybody know we're all right— and on the way we'll get those jam puffs we talked about. And then for heaven's sake let's start enjoying Nellie's holiday, now that we can. A year of being haunted is quite enough for anybody."

"A year!" said Florence. "Yes, I suppose it is. I ought to have stopped it sooner. Perhaps I could have done, if I'd managed to force the aunts, or somebody, to listen to me."

"You could have stopped it anytime—by thinking about something else," said Louis; but the girls ignored him.

"We did it ourselves, and that was good," said Nellie. "We did what needed to be done. Friends can."

They went on soberly; only Louis's thoughts were entirely cheerful. Louis felt relieved of a responsibility and of a worry, and glad that the two girls were safe from what their own imaginations—as he believed—had created. His mind rested on jam puffs and his mouth watered.

Florence and Nellie were happy at the lifting of their

burden of fear and of secret knowledge, happy at each other's hard-won security. But they both felt a vague sorrow, a vague sense of loss; something was broken, something was gone—something perhaps grown out of. They could only express it by repeating to themselves, "Poor George."

Afterword

A *Haunted Year* is a story that has nagged at my mind since I was about seventeen. I never especially wanted to get to grips with the vague idea that I had then, and work out the details of the plot; on the other hand, the idea would not go away and leave me in peace. In the end, after many years, I felt I had to pin down my first idea and work the book out: for the relief of getting rid of the ghost of a book that was haunting me as much as for the pleasure of making something—which is what usually drives me to write.

As I tried to put the flesh and bones of a book onto my ghostly idea, the idea changed. To start with, the book was a book about death: Florence would "disappear" with George and only ever be seen again by a much younger child (the child who comes into the finished book as Audrey). But as I puzzled over other possible endings to the story, I came to see that it should all be more mysterious than that and that some important questions should be left for the reader to decide. So I never say that George is, or is not, a ghost; I never say where he is when he is not with Florence; and I don't spell out what really happens when Florence's illness is at its worst—how much is delirium, and how much is actual event. These things are for you as the reader to puzzle over, as I did—if you like puzzling! If you don't, I hope you enjoy the story as a straight ghost story.

I never had any doubts, even when the story was an idea not yet pinned down, that it belonged to the period shortly before the First World War—to the time of my parents' childhood (which was also, as it happens, the heyday of the classic English ghost story). To us looking back, this was in England a peaceful, settled time, when the pace of social change was slow (not yet accelerated by world wars and the spread of motor transport). People belonged to clearly defined layers: The rich were also in general "the gentry," the property-owning upper classes. The poor were "the laboring classes," in paid employment of some kind. And there was a middle class, then growing in size and importance, whose men were largely in trade and the professions. The main characters in the book belong to this layer of society: They are not rich, though they keep a few servants. Many of the middle class who had leisure to do it adopted the customs of the rich, spending a lot of time in exchanging visits with one another. Aunt Addy does this; the Gages were once a rich family, and she keeps some old habits. Florence's aunts don't. They actually have an occupation, which their neighbors think eccentric of them. And when Marcus says to Audrey "Doctors' daughters don't ride to hounds"—that is, go fox hunting—he means "We aren't rich and important, so don't go getting ideas!"

There was at that time a wider gap between children and adults than there is today, so that it seems to me credible that Florence should not be able to speak about

George to most of the adults she encounters and that her one serious attempt—when she talks to her father—should be a failure. There was also a wider gap between boys and girls, in that girls were expected (even more than now) to be decorously behaved "little women," and boys were expected to be exuberant, noisy, and brave (in fact, future soldiers). Louis plays up to the aunts when he realizes what kind of schoolboyish tricks they expect of him.

In 1910, when the book begins, my mother was eleven and my father twelve. I drew on things they told me about their childhoods for some of the detail in the book. They both bowled hoops, and my mother went on hoop runs organized by a teacher at her school; and among the things she read at school, *Hiawatha* was one of the favorites. She was one of only two children, although not an only child like Florence, and so with adults quite a lot (her brother had his own friends). The large family in the big house in the country was my father's: He had six brothers and three sisters, and a very jolly time they had of it. But my mother, like Florence, was a shy, imaginative child, who delighted in the telling of stories. This is in many ways her book.